Emily Gale and Nova Weetman are friends and writers. They both live in Melbourne—at the same time—and they love swimming.

Emily's books include the Eliza Boom Diaries, *Steal My Sunshine*, *The Other Side of Summer* and its companion novel *I Am Out with Lanterns*, and *Girl, Aloud*.

Nova has written thirteen books for young adults and children. Her middle-grade books include *The Secrets We Keep*, *The Secrets We Share*, *Sick Bay* and *The Edge of Thirteen*.

emilygalebooks.com
novaweetman.com.au

ELSEWHERE GIRLS

EMILY GALE & NOVA WEETMAN

TEXT PUBLISHING MELBOURNE AUSTRALIA

The Text Publishing Company acknowledges the Traditional Owners of the country on which we work, the Wurundjeri people of the Kulin Nation, and pays respect to their Elders past and present.

textpublishing.com.au

The Text Publishing Company
Wurundjeri Country, Level 6, Royal Bank Chambers, 287 Collins Street, Melbourne, Victoria 3000 Australia

Published by The Text Publishing Company, 2021
Reprinted 2021

Book design by Imogen Stubbs
Cover & internal illustrations by Malgosia Piatowska
Typeset in Stempel Garamond by J&M Typesetting
Photograph of Fanny Durack on p 309 held by the State Library of New South Wales, public domain

Printed and bound in Australia by Griffin Press, part of Ovato, an accredited ISO/NZS 14001:2004 Environmental Management System printer.

ISBN: 9781922330451 (paperback)
ISBN: 9781925923988 (ebook)

A catalogue record for this book is available from the National Library of Australia.

FSC
www.fsc.org
MIX
Paper from
responsible sources
FSC° C009448

This book is printed on paper certified against the Forest Stewardship Council® Standards. Griffin Press holds FSC chain-of-custody certification SGSHK-COC-005088. FSC promotes environmentally responsible, socially beneficial and economically viable management of the world's forests.

Dedicated to Aidan Fennessy

PART 1

TAKE YOUR MARKS

1

Guilty

It's midnight and I'm alone in the kitchen eating a cold potato scallop. Coach O'Call would say something like *That's not what I expect from a scholarship girl!* because I have to be up for squad training in five hours, I'm not supposed to go near potato scallops, and—oh, yeah—it's my fifth.

I know the consequences, they circle me as I chew, chanting like bullies. *Indigestion! Weight gain! Poor performance in the pool!* But as I suck the grease and salt off my fingertips, a rumour starts to spread that I'm going for lucky potato scallop number six.

Rumour confirmed.

Bite taken.

I promise this is the last one.

Coach O'Call's laminated food list gives me the evil eye from the fridge. There's a *Yes!* column of foods that should make up most of my diet and a *No!* column that sounds like heaven. Potato scallops aren't even on it. They must be worse than bad. The snack of outcasts and criminals.

Cat Feeney, you are charged with the crime of not taking your swimming scholarship seriously. How do you plead?

I stare out into an imaginary courtroom.

Coach O'Call and Dad would take turns being the prosecuting lawyers: *Isn't it true that you binge-watched Netflix instead of getting an early night before your training session?*

My sister Maisy would race to the witness box to give evidence against me: *Cat doesn't deserve a scholarship. She only pretends to eat salad!*

Mum's away a lot for work so she'd FaceTime to let the court know she's on my side: *I blame the potato scallops! FREE CAT FEENEY!*

I could argue that it's not my fault that we had cold potato scallops in our kitchen in the first place; it's because Dad runs the mini-mart downstairs and cooks more than he can sell.

I could argue that other thirteen year olds commit crimes a lot worse (*actual* crimes).

I could argue that I didn't ask to come to Sydney, that I never wanted to leave my old life in Orange behind, and that I didn't even want a swimming scholarship at stuck-up Victoria Grammar.

I creep down the narrow hall towards the room I have to share with my sister, past Dad's bedroom (he's snoring, Mum's at work), past the bathroom (I should brush my teeth but I keep going). In our room, Maisy's in bed on the far side, wearing a sleep mask. Perfect, salad-loving Maisy, who would never eat six potato scallops at midnight. She makes me want to be bad. Before I know it I'm improvising a terrible dance in her honour: I jump and jerk and kick up my feet, then I bend over—bum-wiggle bum-wiggle—*whoops!* A fart.

Sorry, Maise. Dancing isn't the best idea after salty cold potato.

In bed, I stare at the blank wall on my half of the room. It's been months since we moved but my stuff is still in a box in the corner, along with Aunt Rachel's junk (she's an eBay addict). Swimming trophies, medals, posters, strips of photobooth pictures of me with my friends back in Orange. I can't make the room mine because I don't want it to be. I feel flat and lonely now. I miss home so much.

Last year Dad's building company went broke and we lost everything. When my Aunt Rachel offered him her shop in Surry Hills because she was going to live overseas, my parents decided on a fresh start in Sydney. So Dad's a shopkeeper now, and we live upstairs where it's poky and dark. Dad's doing his best but the shop is small and grimy and a lot of the people around here turn their noses up when they walk past.

Mum is allowed to escape all the time because she's a flight attendant. Maisy, who's in the year below me, is all 'Orange who?' She loves our new school and since she made the swimming squad a few weeks ago she's been painfully cheerful.

I'm the only one who doesn't like our new life. And that's the worst for a few reasons. I fought for the swimming scholarship even though I didn't really want it, just to be a winner. But now what? Coach O'Call wears a black stopwatch around her neck that times us to one-hundredth of a second. So much depends on these tiny fractions of time.

One hundred times less than a second.

Less than a blink of the eye.

I see those stopwatch numbers climbing in my dreams.

My scholarship is the only reason that Mum and Dad can afford to send us both to Victoria Grammar. And after losing everything, the scholarship letter was the first thing that made Dad light up. He cried happy-parent tears. Killer.

So I plead guilty, of course (back in my imaginary courtroom). No matter how angry or sad I get about leaving my old life behind, guilty is the way I feel when I don't behave like a scholarship girl.

My tummy gurgles like a blocked sink. It's less than five hours until I have to be in the pool.

2

Laps

By the time Mina trounces through the turnstile towards the changing rooms with her hair ribbons and her school uniform, I've swum over a hundred laps. I wish she'd hurry so we'd have time for a race. Ma doesn't like it when I'm late back. Swimming has to fit in around all my chores: there are rabbits to skin, floors to scrub, clothes to mend—and that's just on Mondays.

Heading back across the belly of the baths, I start swimming breaststroke. It's not my favourite stroke, but I want to improve my times. My arms pull through the water. My legs shoot me forward.

On my fourth lap of breaststroke my left ankle is grabbed. I hear Mina's laugh, so I wrench my leg free and power to the end of the pool as fast as I can. The fingers of my left hand touch the rough stone edge, and Mina slams into the wall alongside me. She bursts out of the water with a grin and pushes her hair back off her face.

'Bit slow today, Fan,' she says.

I pull a face at her because this is what she does: turns up late when I'm starting to get tired and then teases me. I try not to fall for it, but swimming is the one thing I never find amusing.

'Dad said you've been here all afternoon,' she says.

'Longer than you anyway,' I tell her, tucking my hair behind my ear.

'Trying to get in some training so you will beat me on Sunday,' she says cheekily.

I splash water into her face. 'I don't have to train to beat you.'

'You do so, Fanny Durack. You have not won a single race this year,' she says.

I wish it wasn't true. It's not like I haven't been training harder than anyone. 'I'll beat you, Mina Wylie. Just you wait.'

I push my toes into the squelchy seaweed on the bottom of the baths, wishing a giant wave would come and drag Mina out to sea. Then I wouldn't need to beat her.

'I'm only late because I had to go to school. You're so lucky you don't have to,' she tells me.

'You're so lucky you don't have to scrub the floors or skin the rabbits.'

Mina pretends to shudder. '*Ew*, skinning rabbits.'

I lean in close and drop my voice. 'Actually I like skinning rabbits. Peeling the furry skin down around their warm bodies and then twisting and pulling them free.'

Half laughing and half squealing, Mina pins me by the shoulders and pushes me under. I throw her off and burst up and out. I've long forgiven Mina for her life of leisure, but I still like winding her up. All she has to do is learn needlework and swim. And she struggles to take that as seriously as her father would like.

Mina likes saying that Mr Wylie built these baths especially for her. Imagine having a father who could afford that. My family scrape together the entrance fees for my races. Mina lives just up the hill in a large house in Coogee with a view of the sea, but I have to travel all the way from grimy Surry Hills by tram. On a bad day it can take hours and that means Ma's wrath if I miss the chores. It's hard but it's worth it. Even on a cold day when the air is crisp and the sun is hidden, the water is clear and salty, and nobody tells me to stop training if a man is swimming in the baths too. At any of the other baths I can only train if it's a women's swimming morning, because the NSW Women's Swimming Association thinks that men should not see us in our bathing suits. They say it's immoral. I say it's swimming.

'Race you back, Fan!'

Before I can answer, Mina's gone, her strong arms churning through the water. I take off after her.

I rush in through the front bar of our pub. It's crowded with men drinking beer and talking loud. My long hair is still damp from the water, and some of the men gape as I pass—women are not often seen in here. I'm not fussed by their comments, because I'm still imagining the cheers of the crowd on Sunday as my hand touches the end of the baths before any of the others. As I weave through the men, Da fixes me with a cross look, but it fast disappears. He rarely stays angry. Unlike Ma, he wants me to swim. He glows with pride whenever I do well. He even clips all the mentions of my name from the pages of the paper and pins them up behind the bar.

'You're late, Fan,' he shouts over the din.

'Sorry, Da. I was swimming so fast that I forgot the time,' I shout back.

He raises an eyebrow, and I know what it means. I nod. 'Really, really fast, Da.' I don't mention that Mina beat me easily. But it was her second lap for the day, and at least my hundredth. Mr Wylie has purchased a new-fangled timepiece that marks our times in the pool as accurately as the ones they use at carnivals. Mina doesn't like her father timing me. She wants to be the only swimmer who knows her daily times.

Da smiles broadly. 'Shame you're so determined in the baths, but not so in the kitchen.'

'I'm going, I'm going,' I tell him, ducking through the narrow gap in the bar. I give him a kiss on his rough cheek and I hurry upstairs. The smell of rabbit cooking is so strong that it makes my stomach rumble with hunger.

The noise of my family is bubbling over in the tiny rooms where we live, and I try to get past the kitchen without being seen.

'Fanny Durack, you come back here,' shouts Ma.

I lean my head around the edge of the doorframe, hoping she'll find my funny face amusing.

'Where've you been then, Fanny?'

'Swimming,' I tell her.

'I never would have thought it. Here I was thinking poor Fanny's downstairs mucking out the swill, and all this time you were at the baths.'

'The tram was late, Ma.'

'Seems that particular tram is often late when it's carrying you. And Kathleen had to do the dinner. Again,' she says, stirring the large pot that's simmering over the coals of the oven.

'I'll make it up,' I say, knowing that will involve a lot of work because my sister Kathleen detests skinning rabbits.

'And your hair is wet. You'll catch your death. I'm not caring for this swimming business, Fanny. It's taking you away from your chores and your family.'

Behind me, my younger sister Dewey slides her hands around my waist and leans in against my back. 'You smell like the sea,' she says quietly.

Dewey is the sweetest member of my family. Not yet thirteen and kinder than kind. The others are a mixed bag. John's the eldest, then there's Thomas—off seeking his fortune at the moment—then Kathleen and Mary, my brother Con and me in the middle, followed by Dewey, Mick and little Frankie. One bedroom for the girls and one for the boys—not to mention one *rule* for the girls and something else entirely for our brothers.

'Be gone with you both,' snaps Ma. 'Go and help Kathleen bring up the wood.'

I spin around, pulling a silly face and making Dewey laugh. We run down the stairs, and I tell her how fast I was today and how I could have swum to England.

Outside, Mick brings the axe down as I burst through into the tiny yard. The log splits. I wait for him to step back.

'My turn.' I reach for the long wooden handle.

'You'll cut your leg off,' yells Mick, trying to reach it before me.

'Or yours,' I yell, raising the axe and letting it fall

13

down hard on another log, while Dewey cheers me on. I split wood as well as any boy, but Kathleen shakes her head at me.

'Put it down, Fanny,' she says. 'Chopping wood is not a lady's job.'

'How fortunate that I'm not a lady!' I say lightly, but I drop the axe and help her collect the chopped wood in her skirt, because I don't like to upset Kathleen. She works harder than any of us girls. And she often does my chores too. I have other thoughts in my head of swimming and competing that don't involve being a lady.

'I'll do the fish on Sunday,' I tell Kathleen. 'And the washing. I promise.'

She looks up at me and I see a smudge of dirt under her eye. 'And?' she says.

'More? Really?'

She nods, keeping her smile under control.

'Fine then, and I'll brush your hair.' This is the worst trade, because we have to do a hundred strokes every night.

'Deal,' she says, grabbing a firm hold of each side of her skirt and heading back up the stairs with the wood.

'She played you for a fool,' calls Dewey over the sound of the axe.

'I'll be swimming on Sunday,' I say with a laugh. 'I

think I played her!'

'I heard that,' calls Kathleen from the top of the stairs.

I wink at Dewey, and she grins at me. Sunday can't come fast enough.

3

Squad

Cheep-cheep! Cheep-cheep! Cheep-cheep!

'Cat! Time to wake up!'

It can't be. Maisy sets her cheeping-chicken alarm for 4.55 am, and from 4.56 am all I hear is, 'Time to wake up! time to wake up!' As if I don't already know that it's time to wake up, because when you're in squad it is *always time to wake up.*

'Cat...*Cat*...'

'Shut up, Maise! My alarm hasn't gone off yet.'

Mine is set for 5.05 am. We need to leave at 5.10 am to get to training on time. The way I feel right now, that's impossible. I've literally never felt this tired.

Maisy turns on the light.

'Hey!' I yell.

'Where's my left Croc, Cat? You've taken it, haven't you?'

Here we go.

'Why would I do that?'

'I don't know! Because you're the worst sister ever? Tell me where it is!'

'Turn out the light, Maisy, I've still got six minutes.' I put a pillow over my face.

Maisy makes a frustrated grunt and I hear her rummaging in our wardrobe and then in Aunt Rachel's box of eBay junk. 'I can't find it! I hate you, Cat,' she hisses as she leaves the room.

I peer out from the pillow and spy one yellow Croc on top of the wardrobe.

School is in Coogee, a fancy beach suburb half an hour away by bus. Dad drives us there for training every morning and we make our own way home in the afternoon.

I force down two bananas and try to brush my teeth with a blob of toothpaste on the end of my finger. The three of us are quiet in the car. We used to have a much nicer one. This car belonged to Dad's cousin and sat in his driveway for years. His cat had a litter of kittens in it, but we didn't get to keep one. It's a dirty yellow colour with one blue door, and it smells of cigarettes and cat wee and makes dying noises. Good job it's usually dark when Dad drops us off at Victoria Grammar so no one sees it. Dad says he doesn't care, but since he lost his business he's different.

I think he secretly hates working in the mini-mart. Maybe that's the real reason I ate the potato scallops last night, so that he wouldn't look at them and think I've lost my job, my home, my car…and nobody wants my potato scallops.

Dad stoops to look at the sky through the wind-screen. 'That's your mum's plane coming in to land,' he says.

I feel lighter at the thought of hugging Mum after school. Then I get a tight sensation in my chest as I imagine telling her what I've been thinking lately: that I'm bored of squad and wish I'd never won a scholar-ship. Mum and Dad won't ever want to hear that.

The junior squad—twenty of us—stands in front of the whiteboard studying the drills Coach O'Call has written on the board. First the warm-up, followed by 4 x 100m at race pace. Then 6 x 50m with a kickboard, 5 x 100m of different strokes, 5 x 100 pull (which means no kicking), and a final drill of 10 x 50m sprints. One and a half hours of hard swimming that doesn't get you anywhere except back where you started.

The bananas I ate haven't gone down yet. I need to do a massive burp but nothing's coming out, which is a shame because I'd love to see the look on Rebecca

Jeffers' face. She's in squad and we aren't exactly friends. Though we swim roughly the same times in training, in races I beat her nine times out of ten. And we're both on the relay team but I swim the final leg, the position always given to the fastest swimmer. Last week at training, my time slipped. I knew it from Coach O'Call's expression as she looked at her stopwatch. Then she wrote the times on the board. Rebecca made a huge deal out of it and said in her slimy way, 'Maybe Cat and I should swap places for this Saturday's relay, Coach.' I managed to convince Coach to leave us where we are, but Rebecca will try again. She's a coldwater crocodile snapping at my heels.

'Okay, sleepyheads, get in the water before I chuck you in!' shouts Coach O'Call. She can be a real gorgon and some of the girls are scared of her. She's old and tanned with a wrinkled face like one of those adorable dogs. I've never seen her wear anything other than a white tracksuit. She has a prosthetic leg. She takes it off to swim. Some days she gets around in a wheelchair. She's won three Paralympic gold medals and six silver in freestyle. None of us has ever beaten her in a freestyle race.

After the warm-up, I dive in for the set of timed laps. As usual I'm the pacesetter for my lane, which consists of the six elite swimmers of junior squad.

My first lap always feels amazing, no matter what. I'm a marine mammal, I breathe better when I'm in the water. But as I tumble turn and push off for the second lap, a feeling creeps over me: the numbness I've started to dread. Stroke-stroke, breathe, stroke-stroke, breathe—it's like I'm watching myself do it and wondering, what's the point?

Over the warbly sounds of the water rushing into my ears I can hear Coach yelling. I imagine her pressing that button on the stopwatch—either one hundredth of a second too slow, or one hundredth of a second better than last time—I don't want to think about the numbers. I'm mesmerised by the strands of light on the bottom of the pool that come from the skylight. They twist and turn, making pictures: shimmery seaweed and coral reef. I've never swum in the ocean. Open water. Freedom. No walls or ticking watch. A world away from Victoria Grammar. I pretend I'm there now and that the water is salty instead of so heavily chlorinated that it could dissolve the bodies of the entire squad.

Dolphins swimming beside me. Nodding at me, trying to tell me something. *Cat! Cat!* What is it, Flipper?

'CAT! CATH-ER-INE!'

That's not a dolphin, that's Coach and she sounds cranky. I reach the side and lift my goggles over one eye to see what's happening. Coach and all the elites are at the other end. I've stuffed up the drill. If the pacesetter loses focus it destroys the whole set.

Swimming back to them is a lap of shame.

'What's wrong?' I say innocently.

'You were off pace,' says Rebecca. She looks hungry for blood.

'We haven't got time for daydreaming, Cat,' says Coach.

Great, she can literally read my mind underwater.

'Do I need to remind you that the heats for State Championships begin this afternoon? Start the drills again. I'll have your heat groupings on the board by the end of the session.'

As she walks away, Rebecca yells after her, 'Shall I set the pace, Coach?'

'Sure,' Coach replies, waving her arm as if she doesn't care as long as someone sets it.

Rebecca flashes her eyes at me before she lowers her goggles and dives in.

4

Jitters

I wake to the sound of *Milk-O* being called in the street under my window and the crunching sound of the wheels of the cart on the gravel, and there is no way I'm going back to sleep. Not this morning. Even with Dewey curled up nice and warm against me. I push her feet off mine and she groans as I roll her over.

'Dewey, it's Sunday,' I whisper, not wanting to wake Kathleen or Mary.

'It's not even light,' she whispers back.

My legs start fidgeting under the blankets, and I imagine they are kicking their way down the baths. Knowing I'll annoy Dewey, but also knowing she won't really mind, I lean across and rip the blankets off us.

'Fan!' she hisses. There's a loud shush from the other bed. So, they *are* awake. They know me well enough to know I can't sleep in on race day. As soon as the birds are up so am I. My body is ready to swim.

'Go back to sleep,' says Kathleen.

'It's our day off,' adds Mary.

'Please,' says Dewey, trying to pull the blankets back.

'Bet the bread's been delivered, come on, Dewey!'

'I get the sole,' she tells me sternly. Dewey and I are always racing for the crusty end piece of the loaf.

I lean across and kiss her softly on the cheek. 'You can even have my jam.'

She smiles and rubs her eyes like she's only a baby. 'Let me guess, Fan, you're excited?'

Laughing, I get out of bed because I can't stand it any longer and lean down to find my slippers. I pull hers out too and pass them over. 'I'm so excited, I fear I'll burst,' I say.

We leave Kathleen and Mary in bed and head out, wrapped in morning gowns and slippers and sharing Ma's favourite blanket around our shoulders, to start the fire for breakfast.

I like morning chores on a swimming carnival day because they settle my nerves. I carry as much wood as I can, even more than Da does when he brings in a load, and I stack it inside near the oven. Dewey has pulled the blanket up so she's just a face peeping out.

'Do you think if I win today I'll make the State team? Do you think I can win the 100 yards and the 150 yards? Or should I just focus on one? Do you think there will be a crowd watching? Do you think Ma will come? Do you—'

'Draw breath, Fanny, before you expire and can't swim at all!'

'Apologies, I'm just—'

'Excited, yes I know.'

'Today's the day, Dewey. I'm going to beat Mina. I can feel it.'

'There's also Gladys and Dorothy and Doris,' says Dewey.

'I know. I'm going to beat them all!'

It's not like I haven't won before. I have. Although not as many times as I'd like.

'A cup of tea this century would be nice, Fanny,' says Dewey.

I remember that I'm supposed to be on fire duty and not daydreaming about swimming. I try to concentrate on building the fire, leaving air pockets for the flames to catch.

'Fanny, stop shuffling!' Dewey says from the table.

'Am I?' I say. I need to be in the water. It's the only thing that calms me down.

Ma walks into the kitchen with the milk. She looks tired. I really hope she comes today to watch me, but I don't feel that I should ask her. If only Da could come and my brothers. They don't have to work today.

Sunday is their day off. If only the association would allow men to see us in our bathing suits, then they could come too. Da would cheer louder than anyone in the stands. Even Dewey.

'You're up early, girls,' says Ma. 'Nerves I expect, Fanny. Wake everyone, did we?'

'Yes, Ma, she did!' says Dewey.

I smile and kiss Ma on the cheek, before she ducks away busying herself.

'I have a good feeling about today's race, Fanny,' says Ma. 'I think it might be your turn.'

The smile cracks large across my face before I can stop it. 'I feel it too!' I say.

Ma goes about fixing the fire that I built. It's fry-up day. Our only hot breakfast for the week and Ma likes it just so.

'Cut the bread, Fanny. Dewey, you start on the tea. Bread and dripping all round,' she says. Then she pulls one of her stern Ma faces and growls. 'That blanket's too good to be in here, Dewey Durack!'

'Sorry, Ma,' says Dewey half tripping as she runs out. I smile to myself as I take down the chopping board and the large cutting knife and start on the loaf, feeling the charge of the coming day running through me.

5

Gum

After training, I walk across the sports field with Maisy. All the lucky girls—the ones who don't have to get up at five—are walking in through the main gates. My old friends would die if they saw our straw hats and blazers. *What century are you from?* they'd say.

Maisy scuffs the ground with her shoe. She's the moody one for a change.

I nudge her. 'What's up with you?'

She shrugs. 'We're in the same heat this afternoon.'

'So?'

Maisy glares at me.

'*What*, Maisy?'

'We're sisters and we'll be racing against each other.'

I don't get it so I do the mature thing and ignore her. This is the perfect time to squeeze in some text messages to my friends back in Orange. After a while I realise that Maisy isn't walking beside me anymore.

At the front of the main building there are huge pillars wrapped in ivy. Grey stone gargoyles look down on us. The huge door makes me feel like I'm walking into a museum. I miss the ramshackle portables of my old school, where I didn't feel anxious about breaking something or talking too loudly.

Maisy and I didn't have much to do with each other back in Orange. Our bedrooms were at opposite ends of the house, and she was still at primary school when I started high school. Now it's same school, same bedroom, same swimming regime. She's always there.

Except for right now, obviously. Maybe a gargoyle carried her off.

Suddenly the face I look forward to seeing at school is right in front of me. Lucy: my only Sydney friend.

'Did you bring it?' she says anxiously.

'Bring what?' I fake confusion. Lucy and I are paired for a science assignment and she messaged me twice last night to remember my part.

Here comes the explosion.

'The science homework! It's due today, Cat!'

I smile.

'You total fungus, Cat! I just lost all feeling in my legs.' She punctuates her words with a few light hits to my shoulder.

'You seriously cannot punch, Luce,' I say.

'Shush, I'm a thinker. It's all up here.' Lucy taps her temple and walks briskly to our lockers. She never wastes time, she's always focused on schoolwork. Lucy is a scholarship girl like me. They tested her brain instead of how fast she can swim and the results came in: super brainy. But she isn't boring, she's funny and down-to-earth and messy: I love her wild hair and untucked shirt, like she hasn't got time for the uniform rules. Her hair takes more than three hair elastics to contain it. I have a pixie cut. I got sick of tangled chlorine-hair. Lucy's skin is a warm brown colour, whereas I've got Dad's Irish skin and get sunburnt under a bedside lamp.

'Isn't it the State heats this week, Cat?'

'First one's this afternoon.'

'Nervous?'

'Dunno. My times have been a bit off. It's like I've forgotten the point of swimming.'

Lucy frowns as she puts her locker key around her neck. 'I thought the point was to win. Though you also said the point was to beat Rebecca.'

'Did I?' I probably did, but I don't feel it in every muscle the way I used to.

'Here, take this.' Lucy hands me a piece of chewing gum.

'Does my breath smell?'

'No, but gum has been scientifically proven to improve memory. It'll help you *remember* the point of swimming.'

I laugh. 'You're a tragic nerd.'

'I'm your friend,' she says, solemnly. 'I want you to win.'

'Okay, stop. You're freaking me out.'

Lucy giggles and goes cross-eyed. She works harder than anyone I know. It's partly because she has to get good marks, just like I have to keep winning races, but I think that's who she is, scholarship or not. Her dream is microbiology. I've don't know anyone who fantasises about identifying cells like Lucy.

'See you in science,' she says, hurrying off.

I call out, 'We have science today?'

She shakes her head without looking back, but I bet she's smiling.

The first-round heats are a cinch. I feel like the old me again. Maybe my lazy phase is over. Maybe the chewing gum worked! All I know is that I can't wait to get home and tell Mum that I'm through to the next heat for the State Championships. It's only been a couple of days but it feels like ages since I saw her.

I'm on a high on the bus home, up the back with a window seat. I put in my earbuds and choose a playlist.

Maisy's next to me, reading a book. She hasn't said a word. She came third so maybe she's sulking, but third is good for Maisy, it means she's still in with a shot at State. I'll try to remember to tell her that later. I prefer it if people just leave me alone when I'm in a bad mood.

Close to the last stop, I feel my phone vibrate. Maisy gets her phone out too.

Sorry, girls. Have to fill in for a colleague on a flight to Rome. I'd say no, but you know the situation. Won't be back for a couple of days. Take care of Dad, and each other. I love you so much. Mum x

I was so happy a second ago but now I feel like crying. Mum can't turn work down—so many flights were cancelled because of the virus—but I hate it when she's gone. I angle myself away from my sister and stare out the window.

'Tuna alla Papa,' Dad announces, putting a dish on the table.

Maisy giggles. 'We're not Italian, Dad.' She puts her nose into the steam rising from the plate.

'All right, have it your way: tuna pasta bake. You serve, Maise, I'll get the veg. You're quiet tonight, Cat. Thought you'd be full of beans after winning today.'

He puts a bowl piled high with green beans in front of me and makes a silly face.

'Eh? Eh? *Beans*, get it?'

'That's hilarious, Dad,' I say without twitching a single facial muscle.

I let Maisy and Dad do the talking at dinner and quietly pick the sweetcorn out of the pasta bake. I wish Mum was here. I keep checking the clock on the wall, thinking that it's only two hours until I'm supposed to be asleep so that I'm fresh for another round of squad. I'd like to snap the hands off that clock. *Tick tick tick*. There's never time to do anything I want to do. Even worse, I'm not even sure what that is!

After dinner I leave Maisy stacking the dishwasher, head to our bedroom and shut the door. I need space.

My sister walks in before I've even kicked off my shoes. I groan and flop on the bed.

After a while I hear her rummaging around in the boxes. 'Don't touch my things,' I warn her.

'I'm not, I'm having a look at Auntie Rachel's eBay stuff. Look at this weird thing. It's a glass slide like we use in Science and it's got some short hairs on it.'

'Let me see.' There's a label on brown card that says *Hairs of a sea-mouse. Mounted in carbolic acid, 1887.* 'What's a sea-mouse? I bet Lucy knows, I'll ask her.'

Maisy looks through the box while I text Lucy. 'Cat, look at this! An old stopwatch.' She sits on my bed next to me and puts it to her ear. 'Not ticking.'

It looks solid and silver but it could use a polish. It's stopped at three forty-five. The minute hand and the skinny timer hand are lined up together on the nine, and the shorter hour hand is nearly on the four.

'It looks like someone diving off the block,' says Maisy. 'The two long hands are the legs and the hour hand is the body. I bet it was used to time races in the olden days.'

'There are other things in life, you know. Can you get off my bed?'

Maisy tuts but she gets up and stands in the middle of the room. She's winding the top of the stopwatch. Then she gasps.

'I think I've broken it.'

'*Maisy!* Why'd you do that?'

She spins to face me. 'You don't even care about it!'

'Yes I do. Give it to me before you break it even more.' I take it straight out of her hand. She looks too guilty to fight me for it, and leaves the room. I put the broken stopwatch next to my bed and check my phone to see if Lucy has replied. She's sent me a photo of a fuzzy looking worm. *Sea-mouse: a marine worm that lives on the bottom of the ocean. They're cute!*

I knew Lucy would know.

Dad calls out to ask if I want to watch something on TV with them, but I stay where I am.

Later, after Maisy has gone to bed and turned her light out, I notice the stopwatch again. The thinnest hand—the timer—is ticking backwards, very fast. Whatever Maisy did has made the stopwatch go the wrong way. I get into bed, holding it. I can't stop watching it spin around and around, anticlockwise. It's making me dizzy. I try to blink the feeling away but it won't stop. I feel a bit sick, or am I imagining it?

I can't look anymore. I drop the stopwatch onto a pile of clothes next to my bed, and turn out the light.

6

Race

The tram is so full; we girls have to fight for a spot. Ma's with us too. All five of us cramped without a seat to share. I couldn't sit down anyway. Now we're heading to Lavender Bay, my heart has started to gallop like it does on a swim carnival day. I'm so glad Ma is here. She sometimes can't spare the time to come and watch.

I have the tuppence for my entry tight in my hand. Ma wanted to carry it for me, but I didn't want to let it go. I know I won't lose it. The others chatter on about Annette Kellerman in Boston. She was arrested on the beach for wearing the type of bathing suit made for men. It sounds as if America is even more old-fashioned than here. Annette Kellerman is my idol, but I can't be lost in all that now. I have to stay on track.

This race is one of the first for the season. Our times will count in determining who represents the state at the Australasian championship carnivals to be held in

Brisbane in March. I have to win one of my races or at least place close to the winner to have a chance.

'Look, Fan!' says Kathleen.

The others are looking out the back of the tram at a man chasing his dog down the street. The dog is running in circles with a string of sausages hanging from its mouth. My sisters all start laughing. Even Ma can't resist.

'Run, little dog,' I call out.

'Run!' adds Dewey.

The tram swings around the corner and we lose sight of the dog. Dewey leans against me, her mood all light. 'I think it's a sign, Fanny! You're going to be as fast as that little dog today.'

'You calling me a dog, Dewey?' I ask playfully.

'It's our stop next, girls,' says Ma. She seems nervous. She's clutching her handkerchief and twirling it between her fingers. I'm not used to seeing Ma worry about my swimming.

The brakes of the tram grind against the metal and it pulls up at the stop. I follow my sisters off and take in the sweet warm air. Now that the sun is up, I can tell the day is going to be perfect.

Lavender Bay Baths are my favourite. There's a wooden tower for the high-diving display and space for many onlookers. And there are funny races and walking the greasy pole. We have to take the steam ferry across from the point, and that's the best way to arrive.

I squeeze into the corner seat on the outside deck of the ferry. Dewey is with me. The others are inside, out of the wind. We always nab this perch if we can because it's the best view of the baths and the hill and the people.

'What will you buy with your winnings?' asks Dewey.

'Winnings! Only the men win money, remember. We win things like hairclips and vouchers.' I grin at Dewey whose hair is coming unclipped and flying behind her in the breeze. 'Besides, I haven't won yet.'

'You will.'

There are thousands of women and young ladies pressed tight in the stands at the baths. There's a certain feeling in the air as we walk through the crowd. Ma grips my hand tighter than tight. I can feel her skin all rough and worn, and it makes me want to win even more.

Kath and Mary are judging the earlier races and have hurried off to their duties. I'm not on for a bit, so I can watch Dewey in her wading race.

'Can you come to the dressing room with me?' Dewey asks.

'Of course!'

Ma leaves us to go and find our aunt in the stand. And I follow Dewey to the dressing room. My legs are so jittery I could dance my way there.

'Look, there's Dorothy!' Dewey points into the crowd.

Dorothy waves from where she sits in the stand with her family. I wave back enthusiastically. I'm glad Dorothy is here. She's one of the strongest swimmers around and if I'm going to prove myself then I need to beat swimmers like her. She's been talking about going professional so she can earn money by winning races, but that would mean she couldn't swim at the Olympics one day. Not that girls are allowed to swim at the Olympics. I hold a secret hope that one day things will change. But I keep it quiet.

'Fanny! Keep up,' shouts Dewey. I skip along the boardwalk to catch up to her. There are just so many people here. I'm wishing now that I listened to Ma and ate my bread and dripping earlier this morning. My stomach is whirling and wriggling like there's a giant fish in there waiting to get out.

The dressing-room attendants know Dewey and me, so we slip through without any problem. I wait for Dewey in the washroom while she goes through to change. I've been trying to talk her into swimming in the proper races, but she says she likes the wading events best because there's not so much pressure. She says she's happiest watching and cheering for me. Dearest Dewey.

'The water's going to be very chilly today, Fan,' Dewey says, traipsing out in her costume. The long thick itchy wool hangs loose on her small frame. I tower over her. She has Ma's body. I have Da's: strong, muscular and tall.

'Tie my hair back for me?' she asks.

I start separating her hair so that I can plait it. It's not neat like Kathleen would do and she keeps pulling away, making me yank it even more.

'Ow!'

'Sorry, but there are knots. You didn't brush it this morning, did you?'

'I didn't have time. I had to sweep out the yard while you were getting ready!'

Guiltily, I try to plait the rest more gently. 'There. Done!'

She reaches back to feel the job I've done. 'Do you want me to do yours?' she asks.

I shake my head. 'No chance. I like the feel of it floating around my face. Come on. Your race will be over before we even make it into the baths.'

We walk out to the start end of the baths. The noise has started to grow. I lean down and scoop my fingers through the water.

38

'You're right! It's quite fresh,' I tell Dewey. 'Wade fast and you'll warm up! I'll be watching from the end.'

I head for the stands. Mina should be around somewhere. And Gladys. Usually we all sit together cheering on the swimmers in the events before us, but today Mina's performing with her father and her brother in some high-diving exhibition and I'm not sure where she is.

I can't find Ma either, so I stand close to the water as the gun is fired and Dewey's race starts. It's over quickly and Dewey places second, which she'll be happy with.

'Second place, might be a sign,' says a voice behind me and I know it's Mina.

'Aren't you showing off on the diving board?' I say sharply.

'Not until after I beat you in the pool!'

I can't help but laugh, and Mina joins in. It's always like this before a race. Mr Wylie thinks it helps us get in the mood for a competition, but Ma doesn't like it at all. She worries it's unladylike.

'Is Gladys here too?' I ask.

'Somewhere, no doubt. She's not going to miss this race.'

It's been the five of us forever: Gladys, Doris, Dorothy, Mina and me. There are others too but we are the most serious.

'Watch Dorothy today, especially in the 50 yards. Her times are improving,' says Mina. 'Dad says she's a strong contender.'

Mina's father is a champion long-distance swimmer and he thinks he can recognise champions just by watching them train. He's been right before about some of the swimmers who train at Wylie's Baths, and I know Dorothy is a threat today.

'I'm going to change,' I tell Mina.

'I'll come too,' she says.

I wish she wouldn't. I'd like five minutes to myself, just to get my head right, but Mina trots along beside me saying hello to people as we pass the crowds. She's a favourite here. They've been watching her perform tricks with her hands tied together underwater since she was five.

Nobody much notices me. That's all about to change.

Mina chatters at me while we pull on our bathing suits, but I ignore her. She's used to me being silent before a race.

I remain quiet while we walk to the other end of the baths. Our race is up next. Mina starts chatting to the other bathers, but I stare down into the water. It's murky and dark.

We bunch together on the edge of the platform waiting for the gun. I'm wedged between Mina and

Dorothy. The crowd is hushed, like they know it's going to be an exciting race.

I tug my long hair back and smooth it with my hands. Then I focus on the water in front of me. I need a neat dive and strong strokes. I need to get right out in front from the start, because coming from the back can be hard.

I take one big deep breath to steady myself.

The gun fires.

We dive. I come up in front and start hard, arms and legs powering through the water. Each time I turn my head for air, I hear the cheer from the crowd. My eyes sting with the salt but I force them open, knowing if I close them for a second I'll swim off track and bump into one of the others. I need to swim straight. It's the fastest.

I can sense Dorothy at my shoulder. She's inching up closer. Mina too. But I'm still in front. My legs feel strong, like they could kick forever.

The end of the baths is close now. I keep stroking fast. But Dorothy's gaining on me. Head down, head up, breathe in, breathe out. My arms loop over and into the water propelling me forward. Twenty strokes left. Fifteen. Dorothy's alongside me.

Ten. There's Mina. She's close too.

Five. I can do this. My fingers are reaching for the

wall. I kick the water hard.

I glide in, slam the edge.

But Dorothy and Mina are there first.

I've lost.

7

Wagging

I've been lying awake for ages, unable to switch off my brain. Now I finally feel like I could drift back to sleep, but Maisy's cheeping chicken is a major threat.

Please let me sleep, chicken...

Cheep-cheep! Cheep-cheep! Cheep-cheep!

I squeeze my eyes shut just before Maisy turns on the light. Despite an early night and no salty cold potato snacks...I just *can't* get up.

Maisy gets ready in silence. No sweet voice urging me to get out of bed and no accusations either (good, she hasn't noticed that I used the last of her strawberry shampoo). The door creaks as she leaves.

Dad and Maisy will be in the kitchen by now, sharing a pot of tea and agreeing about things. Those two are always agreeing about things.

Next thing I know, Dad flings the curtains open as if it's not 5 am and pitch black outside.

'Morning, sleepyhead!'

I make a snap decision.

'Morning, Dad,' I whisper in a scratchy voice. Dad tilts his head so our faces are aligned.

'Come on, Cat, five minutes until we leave.'

'I'm not well.' I pretend it's hard to swallow.

He bends closer.

'My throat hurts. And my head,' I say.

'You can't miss training, Cat.'

I'm crushed that his first thought is training and not my health. I'm faking, but that's not the point.

'I just don't want to push it, Dad. State trials and everything.'

I can't believe I'm doing this. I've never missed training.

Maisy comes in wearing her school tracksuit, hair pulled back in a slick ponytail. 'You're still in bed? Coach hates it when we're late.'

I ignore her and put all my energy into making my eyes look watery while Dad looks deeply into them.

'You do look a bit off,' he says. 'Stay in bed today. We need her at her best for the next heats, don't we, Maise? I'm going to the wholesalers after I drop Maisy at training. Will you be all right here by yourself?'

'I think so.'

'Okay, love. And if you feel better later could you

fold the clean washing like you were meant to? I have to open the shop. I can't do everything, Cat.'

'Sorry, Dad. I promise.'

I'd forgotten about that: instead of doing my jobs after dinner, I hid the laundry basket behind the sofa. I'm passionately against housework.

Once they've gone I slide under the doona, stretch my toes and smile because I got away with it. Time to myself on dry land is rare. I reach under the bed for my phone to check the group-chat of my friends in Orange.

Forty-two messages while I was sleeping! I scroll too quickly to take them in, feeling more left out than ever. My friends don't have to get up at 5 am so they message at night. It means we never really have a conversation. If I reply now they'll hate me for waking them up.

A truck stops outside the shop and loudly empties the recycling bins. It's 5.15 am, and there's just me and the rubbish collectors. What am I doing? Why would I skip training when I just swam the fastest in my heat and might be going to State?

Can anyone tell me why I don't care anymore?

New disaster. Message from Lucy at 6 am: *Don't forget my copy of* Romeo and Juliet. *And no faking this time cos I'm not falling for it, dirtbag! X*

I borrowed Lucy's copy because I've lost mine. She hates not having her books for school so I'll have to go in. I get dressed and write a note for Dad so he doesn't worry when he gets home. *Feeling a bit better. Went to school so I don't get behind.*

There's still plenty of time so after that I make a huge breakfast: scrambled eggs and spinach on toast. It is a masterpiece. Halfway through eating it I take a photo and send it to Lucy, with a promise that I'll bring *Romeo and Juliet* to school.

Somehow the kitchen has reached a new level of gross and there's a puddle of raw egg on the floor. I try to clean it but the cloth is dripping wet with bits of parsley stuck in it and the egg refuses to let go of the tiles. It stretches like snot. This mess is too much, I don't have the skills!

I picture the swimming pool: the squad doing laps like they're supposed to. Even if I don't want this scholarship, the thought of failing is terrifying. Coach is always telling us that the minute we lose focus, we're finished. I don't want *that* either.

It's still two and a half hours until school starts. When I reach for my phone and click on Instagram, the first image that comes up gives me a genius idea: the beach. Girls at school talk about Coogee Beach all the time—it's meant to be gorgeous. The bus that runs between home and school goes near it.

It sounds funny but this could literally be the solution. Can't I be in charge of my own training? I haven't seen the ocean one single time since we moved here—Mum and Dad have been too busy setting up our new life.

My thoughts take shape: a training session in the ocean. That way I don't have to feel so guilty for wagging. And the ocean is supposed to be good for stress!

I'm excited for the first time in ages. Making a decision for myself gives me the kind of goosebumps I used to get before a race. All of my stuff is piled on the floor next to my bed. I shove everything into my schoolbag: keys, phone, Opal card, purse, towel, cozzie, sunscreen, *Romeo and Juliet*, calculator, laptop.

PART 2

GO!

8

Wylie's

Cat

I get off the bus three stops before school and follow the sign to the beach. Is this still a good idea? My head's a mess again. One minute I'm thinking that Mum and Dad would flip if they knew I was going to the beach alone. Next I'm thinking that they'd be proud of me for taking responsibility for my training schedule.

Then there's the fact that I've got my worst subject for first period: History. Sorry, boring! Let's leave the past in the past. This seems like even more reason to have an adventure before I go to school. Then I'll have something interesting to whisper about to Lucy while we pretend to be fascinated by Ancient Greece.

I walk to the top of a hill and spy a patch of sand. Beyond it is the water. Something about the sight of the waves and the horizon makes me fizz inside. Back home in Orange we had Lake Canobolas for swimming or paddle-boarding, but some of my friends thought the water was gross, and if there's no rain the lake dries up. Even from a distance, I'm falling under the ocean's spell.

The beach is dotted with people sunbaking. A group of older teenage boys is playing volleyball and I wander a bit closer. They're bare-chested and I suppose not bad looking, throwing themselves around the sand like puppies.

'You playing, shorty?' yells one. They're looking at me! I hurry up a shady path under gums and conifers that runs parallel to the beach, and I can hear them laughing. I'm not even short, I'm just thirteen. Stupid rude boys. I'm embarrassed to swim in front of them now.

From the top of the path, the ocean is wide and beautiful. But can I really imagine taking on those waves? Through the trees I see a sign: 'Wylie's Baths. Open every day of the year.' An ocean pool—I know what that is—a bit of ocean walled off to keep the waves out.

I go down some concrete stairs past a white building and a statue of a girl looking out over the water. A sudden shiver makes me trip on the next step, but luckily I recover without anyone seeing. Mum always says 'someone's walked over your grave' when I shiver. But Lucy told me it means you're either cold or feeling extreme emotion, even if you don't know it. It's definitely not cold today.

There's no one else around. All I can hear are waves. At the bottom of the stairs there's a turnstile and it's four dollars to get in. I put the coins on the counter and a woman waves me through.

The baths are way down below. Like I thought, it's a piece of the ocean bricked off into the shape of a swimming pool. Up on wooden stilts is a pavilion with changing rooms and a cafe.

In the changing room I quickly strip off and put on my sports bikini. This is the first chance I've had to wear it, seeing as I spend most of my life in a navy blue one-piece with compulsory school swimming cap.

It's got a lilac and blue boho print with a high-neck top and racing back so it's perfect for training, no matter what the squad rules are. Tam gave it to me as a goodbye present.

I leave my uniform on the bench but I need somewhere to stash my schoolbag because it's got my laptop and phone inside. There aren't any lockers so I bring it with me down the steep wooden steps to the water.

There are rocks that surround the baths and I sit down on one to find my goggles, which always magically make their way to the bottom corner of my bag. My hand touches something cold and I take it out along with my goggles. It's the old stopwatch that I was staring at in bed. I must have scooped it up with all my things. That long, thin timer hand is still spinning anticlockwise. What did Maisy do to it? It doesn't tick seconds; it's faster and smoother. It glides. The strange thing is that I'm already in a trance, like last night: a stopwatch you can't stop watching.

The silver case is warm in my hand now. Behind my eyes the wooziness has started. My head gently rotates.

Stop, Cat.

Watch, Cat.

No, I've got to stop.

I leave it on the rock, stuff my bag between the rocks and out of sight and make my way to the water's edge.

Fan

The only good thing to come out of losing my races yesterday was Mr Wylie letting me borrow his special stopwatch. When I saw him waiting outside the carnival for Mina, I just burst out with the bold request. I know he only agreed because he felt sorry for me and my poor times in the water, and I had to promise to return the watch today. I would have used it yesterday to time myself after the swim carnival but Ma insisted we go straight home.

She didn't know Mr Wylie lent me his watch. She would have said no because she doesn't like relying on others to provide things we cannot afford. But I am sure that I will swim faster if I can check my times.

Because I couldn't tell Ma about the watch, I had to sneak out this morning, and because I needed someone to time my laps in the water, that meant taking Dewey with me. Poor Dewey. She was so sleepy when I nudged her awake this morning, but we needed to leave before anyone in the family woke.

'Penny for them, Fan,' says Dewey quietly as we sit on the tram, my bag on the seat next to me.

I look across at my sister and the worry on her face. 'I need to win, Dewey.'

'You will.'

I wonder how long my family will remain hopeful. I should be beating Mina by now. She touched the wall before Dorothy in the 100 yards and the 150, which nobody would have expected. I'm sure it's because she has her own baths to train in, and her own special time-piece to tell her how fast she's going.

Dewey slides her hand in alongside my arm and I squeeze it against my body. 'You will, Fan,' she says.

We get off the tram and I hurry up the hill, wanting to make it to the baths with enough time left for a handful of laps before I return the stopwatch and we have to rush to get home to help Ma with the chores.

Dewey dawdles behind me.

'Hurry, Dewey. I need to train,' I tell her.

She laughs and lets me pull her along. 'Do you ever *not* want to train?' she asks.

'No.'

'Never?'

I shake my head. 'Actually, that's a lie. Once. Last year when my chest was gruesome with infection.'

'But you trained that day,' says Dewey.

'I know—I had to tell Ma I was better. Do you remember? I had to take the stairs three times and not cough before she'd let me go.'

Dewey bumps against me. 'But why didn't you stay in bed? We never get to stay in bed. You could have laid there for the whole day and had Ma bring you syrup and instead you went swimming in the rain!'

Despite myself, I laugh. She's right. I could have stayed in bed. Looking back, I wish I had, but only because Ma made me drink the onion remedy that should always be avoided. Although, I know I'd do the same again. Training is everything.

We've reached the sign for the steps down to Wylie's Baths and I feel my body loosen, knowing that in seconds I'll be in the cool water, swimming faster than Mina and the others in my head.

'Dewey, take Mr Wylie's stopwatch. Press this button when you shout go, okay?'

I hold out the stopwatch to her, showing her the hand that can be started, stopped and reset to tell how fast I've swum.

'I've never held something so grand, Fan. What if I break it?'

'You won't.'

Dewey cups the stopwatch in her hands, like it's an egg that will crack if she should bump it.

'I want to beat Mina's time from yesterday. But you mustn't fib. You must tell me the honest truth about how fast I am.'

Dewey nods as we head in through the turnstile, and I can smell the sea.

Cat

Old people with deep tans lie around the pool like lizards, and the ocean crashes against the back wall of the pool. The water looks clear and shallow. It's rocky on the bottom and covered in seaweed. Looking from here to the far end I'd say it was fifty metres—perfect for training. I dip my foot in.

And out! *Wow!* This is a terrible idea. The water is so cold it feels like teeth. I'm a creature of heated pools. I'm freshwater, not salt.

But nearby, a wrinkled woman is floating on her back. She looks like a baked potato that's been left in the oven too long. But she's smiling. If she can cope with the cold, I need to get over myself.

I climb down the steps before I can change my mind. *Oh, ah, ee…*I can do this.

My feet search out soft sand but find barnacles and slippery algae. I'm scared of what I'll step on next under the glimmering water. Lucy would have it all under a microscope.

I fix my goggles and plunge in. My heart bursts but the hard part is over. I can see dancing seaweed and tiny shells clustering on the rocks. An actual fish!

Fan

I'm pushing myself as hard as I can, stroke after stroke, imagining I'm in the water alongside Mina and Dorothy. I reach the end of the baths, my fingers grazing the cold stone, and I leap up, looking for Dewey.

'Stop the hand, Dewey!' I call.

'I have.'

'And? It felt fast,' I say, sounding hopeful.

She looks down at me, biting her bottom lip. I know what her expression means. That my time was slow, and she doesn't want to say it aloud.

'I'll go again,' I tell her.

She nods. 'Do you want me to walk down the length so I'm at the other end?'

The other end is the far end where the waves break across the top of wall that holds the sea out. It's not safe for Dewey down there. I shake my head.

'I'll swim down and then I'll race back to you. Faster this time.'

She finds a small smile, and I know how much she wants me to beat my best time. It's almost as important to her as it is to me.

I swim back to the deeper end where the water is colder. And then slick my hair back from my face. My sister is small in the distance. I kick off from the wall, and I swim.

Cat

This is too relaxing, I've got to get into training mode. Swimming freestyle, my fingertips graze the bottom. I kick harder. My rhythm feels strange; I never knew that saltwater could feel so different—or that I could feel so different in it.

When I reach the other side I flip into backstroke— the water isn't deep enough to tumble turn—and watch the clouds shift over me. I keep lapping, back and forth, down in the underwater world and then facing the sky. Each lap is something new. I still feel dizzy but it's probably the bright sun and the freezing water.

I'm into my new rhythm now. I feel fast, I just don't

know *how* fast. I haven't kept track of the number of laps and now I'm worried that too much time has passed—I still have to change and get to school. Only it's so good in here. Give me freedom. Give someone else my place at Victoria Grammar.

One more, I tell myself, and then I'll go to school. I still have that buzzy feeling in my head so it's probably best I get out soon. But for my last lap I try to forget that so I can feel every movement and be part of the water. I stay under, holding my breath, arms by my side and dolphin-kicking.

I know this pool by now. The wall is fifteen metres ahead.

Ten metres. I swim even deeper, shivering at the change in temperature. I blow out some bubbles to stay down longer but as they clear something weird is happening. Maybe I've been under too long. This doesn't feel right. I'm so dizzy and everything is blurred. I'm still moving but my body feels numb. I need to make it stop! I need air!

Fan

My arms slow like they are dragging sand and my head feels light and strange like I've been holding my breath too long underwater. I stop swimming as a shiver flushes through me from head to toe. Pressing my feet into the seaweed, I stand up to take a gulp of fresh air, hoping to lose this odd sensation.

I blink. My eyes are having trouble seeing, and then I realise there's something tight across my face. A strange, hard cover across my eyes. I pull at it hard and it comes free. What is this strange coloured cover for eyes? I let it go and it sinks down into the water.

Holy Mary Mother of God, whose tiny hand is that? Not mine. And what's that ring? It looks like a little silver star, but I've never seen a ring like this in my life. I look down. I can see so much skin! My stomach is exposed.

This is not my body.

Heart galloping, I duck down into the water, squatting on the bottom so that just my head is above the surface. Until I work this out, I have to stay hidden. Ma would die if she caught a glimpse of me and I don't even want to think of what Da would do.

What trick is this? Whose body is this?

I sneak a peek at my arms. The skin is so brown. And my hands feel soft, nothing like how my calloused palms usually are. Slowly I pat my hands down my waist and my legs, but it's not the strong, thick legs that I'm used to. And they are smooth! This is the body of a young girl.

My long, tangled hair is gone. Now I have short hair

like my brothers. Everything else is different too: the day, the light, the coolness of the air.

'Dewey?' I call out. I spin around in the water, looking for her, but there's only a grey-haired woman floating on her back.

'Dewey!' I call again, louder this time, feeling desperate. It looks like Wylie's Baths, but also not like Wylie's Baths. People are sitting on big chairs on the balcony and there are men lying on the rocks, just wearing little pants. I look away, mortified—I mustn't see men like that!

'Dewey!' I shout in a very unladylike manner. I need my sister.

'You right, love?' The woman stands up and I see now that she's wearing nothing on her stomach either. Where is her bathing suit? She's brown and wrinkled like leather and she's walking towards me with a worried face. Is she lost too?

'You okay? Didn't get stung by a jellyfish did you? They have been a bit of a problem lately,' she says, smiling.

'Jellyfish? What? No. I've lost my sister,' I tell her, but my voice sounds fancy like Mina's, nothing like mine at all.

'But I saw you arrive, darl. You came alone.'

I frown. 'Is this Wylie's Baths?'

'Are you okay, love? Bit too much sun? Hit your head? Maybe you should hop out of the pool. Have a rest,' she says in a voice as soft as Ma's is when she's worried.

I let her take my arm but then I realise I can't get out wearing this. What if Mr Wylie sees me? Or Mina?

'Is Mr Wylie here?'

'Mr Wylie? These baths haven't been in the Wylie family for a long time.'

I swallow and turn to look at the woman. She nods, confirming the fact. 'The last Wylie was Mina, and she died in 1984,' she says gently.

I stagger back into the cool of the water, letting it swallow me up. How can that be? Mina's gone. Mr Wylie. My family. Me? Who am I? And if 1984 is in the past, then what year is this?

Cat

I've caught my breath but I still don't feel right. Somehow I've lost my goggles and my eyes sting. That woozy feeling I got underwater has never happened before.

'That was a fast one, Fan!' someone shouts in the distance. There's no one else in the water but me. 'C'mon now, Ma'll skin us!' Squinting into the sun I see a girl about my age sitting on the rocks. But she's dressed like she's raided the old ladies' nighties rack at an op shop.

'Fan!' she shouts again. 'Home time!' Her accent sounds familiar but not Australian. And why does she seem to be yelling at me?

Something's tugging at my scalp—seaweed? No, it's hair! Masses of long brown hair floating around my shoulders, and—*no-no-no*—wait, these aren't my shoulders. What's happening? These hands aren't mine. I turn them in front of my face, not believing what I'm seeing.

This isn't me.

I'm wearing something itchy and waterlogged that comes down to the middle of my thighs. Too scared to scream, or move, I pull at the fabric and make a small scared sound at the back of my throat. What *is* this? I'm Cat. Catherine Isabel Feeney. What else? I'm thirteen, I live in Surry Hills, Sydney, with my dad and my mum and my annoying sister, Maisy. That's who I am, but why do I look like this?

A man walks down some rickety stairs. Those aren't the same stairs I walked down. And where's the cafe? I crouch with the water up to my chin and my teeth chattering. Even my teeth feel different in my mouth.

Is this is a dream? But when did it start? I'm freaking out.

The man yells in my direction, 'Come along, Miss Durack! Looks like bad rain. I'll lose my licence if anything happens to you. Not to mention my head when your father finds out—ha! ha!'

His licence? So he's the owner of the baths. He sounds Irish and I think that girl does, too. But who's 'Miss Durack'? Why are those people yelling at *me*?

I can't just stay in the water. It's so cold now. I start to swim breaststroke to the other side but it's not my body gliding through the ocean bath. *Oh God, oh God*, I whisper onto the surface of the water.

'What's that you're muttering, Fan?' says nightie-girl. She's come to the edge of the pool along with the man. 'Praying to God that Ma doesn't put you on slops duty for being late, are you?' She laughs. I don't. I'm even more terrified. She thinks I'm 'Fan'.

By the time I reach her, my eyes are stinging with tears. 'Excuse me...who's Fan?' I stutter. But that's not my voice, it's Irish too.

The girl giggles and rolls her eyes. 'It's true what we say about her, Mr Wylie. She could have been an actress if she wasn't such a good swimmer. Come on, Fan, out you go.'

I lean on the side, trying to stop myself from passing out.

'Have you hit your head, sister?' she says.
Sister?

After I manage to climb out, I cross my arms over my chest because I've suddenly got the boobs I thought

I wanted—and now I really don't. This body is strange: taller than nightie-girl, older than thirteen. I flinch as the girl puts a thin towel around my shoulders.

'Fan, what is it?' She sounds worried.

What can I say? 'Thanks for the towel.' That's all I can manage.

I notice the man put something shiny that catches the light in one of his pockets, and then he starts to leave. 'Right then, business to attend to. Hope the stopwatch was useful to you, Fanny. Don't be so hard on your-self—your times are competitive and your commitment is—well, swimming on a day like today? I rest my case. See you soon, no doubt.' Then he nods at nightie-girl. 'Good-day, Dewey.'

'Mr Wylie,' says the girl, and bobs her head at him.

Wylie? The sign said Wylie's Baths.

A sudden crack of lightning makes us jump. Nightie-girl pulls me towards the stairs, telling me a storm's coming. But it was a perfect day when I got into the water. This is the weirdest dream I've ever had. I've never wanted to hear Maisy's chicken alarm more than I do now.

'Hurry, Fan, you've got to get changed.'

Yes, changed back into Cat. I need to wake up.

There is no cafe. There are no old people lying next to bottles of sunscreen and takeaway coffees. We get to a changing room but there is no sign of my clothes.

I stand there, stuck and speechless.

'Come on,' says nightie-girl, as if nothing is unusual. She tries to rub my arms through the towel so I step back and turn away from her. Next thing I know, she's passing me clothes. What choice do I have?

I take off the water-logged costume, still shaking. She hands me white baggy knickers and a cotton top like summer pyjamas. Then she puts a stiff top on me and ties it at the back. I think it's a corset; it feels like I'm being winded. Next she hands me stockings that look like they've been worn all week, a long-sleeved shirt with a collar that chokes me, and a skirt so long it's like wearing bedding.

'Here, Fan.' She gives me a delicate cream hairbrush. The hair is heavy and wet down my back, and a feeling builds inside: I'm not me anymore and I'm terrified. With a yell I hurl the hairbrush at the wall and it breaks.

'Fan!' she says, in shock. I turn from her again and then I hear her go to pick up the pieces. 'This isn't like you.'

Fan

I can't stay in the water forever, but I can't let anyone see me like this. I spy some coloured material hanging on the edge of the stairs and make a dash, as fast as if one of my brothers was chasing me, to grab the material and wrap myself as well as I can.

Then I take the stairs up to the changing rooms. I'm terrified that somebody will catch me running like this, which makes me run even faster. I have to dash through the middle of some people who are talking loudly, their voices strange. I notice two ladies sitting on orange chairs. They look like no one I've ever seen. One has bare arms with a painted snake wound round and round her skin, like a sailor. Her hair is very short on one side and then I notice that it's blue. Perhaps she's a performer from the theatre. Then her friend cusses and laughs, and I sprint through the middle, heading for safety.

My heart is galloping as I reach the changing rooms. There are no cubicles for me to hide in. And it's open to the skies and to the world. But at least it's empty. I rush to the mirror by the sink. But it's not me blinking back. It's another face. The mouth drops open. I will it to close. I screw my eyes shut. Not my eyes—someone else's eyes.

I count to five like Ma says I should when I'm trying to stay calm before a race.

But I'm still not me. My long dark hair has gone. I'm younger. Smaller. My nose is straight. My teeth are white. There's nothing left of me.

Except I'm me on the inside. But a stranger on the outside.

So, who am I? And where is my body?

I need to get out of this tiny bathing suit. But my clothes are gone. There's only a grey jacket hanging on the peg and a pile of things folded beneath it. Snap decision, Fanny. I grab the pile of clothes and start dressing.

It doesn't take long to put them on because there are no corsets or extra layers. Just a white shirt and a skirt to my knees. I button the jacket up so that I'm covered as much as I can be. The shoes look too small for my feet, but then I remember my feet are not my feet, so they fit. These clothes must belong to whoever this person is that I am now. I run my fingers through this short hair and like the way it feels.

Now what? Where do I go? I can't go home like this. Ma and Da would have a fit.

And then I remember that if it's some time after 1984, Ma and Da won't be where I left them. I sit down on the warm wooden seat.

I try and swallow, pushing down the fear that is rising in my throat. In the mirror I see an insignia on the pocket of the grey jacket that seems to say Victoria College. I know that school. It's up the hill, away from the beach. These clothes must belong to whoever's body this is. So I need to know who that is. Maybe the school will hold some answers.

PART 3

ENTRY

9

Reflection

Nightie-girl made us get on a strange tram in Coogee. It's open-air at the front and back and looks ready to roll into a museum. We're clattering along, sitting on wooden slatted seats, with just a thin metal arm to stop me from tumbling out. I'm clutching a bag that feels like carpet. Nightie-girl gave it to me as we left the baths. Is this a real bag? Are these real shoes? Is any of this real?

In a dream, can you feel cold air on your face?

The tram is travelling almost the same way that my bus goes. I recognise a few landmarks. This is Sydney, it's just not *my* Sydney.

I can't tell how long it's been since I got out of the water. Every time I let myself wonder about what's happened, my stomach lurches. Did I drown? Am I dead?

'Are you sure you're well, sister?' says nightie-girl.

I open my mouth to reply *I'm not your sister, I'm*

Cat. But instead I nod. I'm scared. It's not just that the voice that comes out doesn't sound like me, but that trying to explain before I know what's happened could make this worse. She hasn't mentioned the hairbrush again. Despite my stuff-ups, somehow she can't see the real me in here. If I go along with things maybe it will wear off. Or I can sneak away and figure out how it happened and how to reverse it.

The tram stops and nightie-girl nudges me to get off. 'Hurry, Fan, we'll be in awful trouble with Ma,' she says. I wish I could remember her name. Back at the ocean baths, Mr Wylie called her something-ooey. I can't think of any names like that. She links arms with me and pulls me across the road in front of a large old car with a single seat at the front, which honks at us.

This is a city of smartly dressed people, vintage cars, carts pulled by horses and trams without doors. It's not that it's noisier than my Sydney, but the noises are different: horses' hooves, tram bells, spluttering engines. I notice what there isn't as well as what there is: no traffic lights, no road-markings, no bright electric shop signs. There are children wandering around without parents, and literally everyone is wearing a hat. Including me.

I know what it all adds up to. This is the past. Could my imagination come up with this, or is it real? Have

I wagged my History class and somehow ended up *in* history?

When we arrive at a three-storey building on the corner of two busy streets, nightie-girl says we're 'home'. I swallow, freshly terrified. The word 'hotel' is painted on one window. It's got one of those fancy wrought-iron canopies. I remember Mum calling that 'lacework' and it sounded strange to me because lace is soft and delicate. Just as we walk underneath the canopy I see a name: Thomas Durack.

I can't go inside; my gut says find home and I think I know the way from here.

'You go in,' I tell her. 'I need to…um…do some stuff.'

'Fan, you're talking strange. Is it Doctor Burke I'll be fetching?' She comes closer.

Maybe she'll leave me alone if I can speak more like her. I try to think of something my nana would say. 'I'm…right as rain, thanks. I've got errands to run.'

'What'll I tell Ma?' she asks, and she sounds worried. 'We'll already be in trouble for leaving this morning without a word.'

'Ma knows all about it,' I reply. I'll say anything to get away.

She frowns but I edge away slowly and finally turn my back on her to make my way up a steep road that looks familiar. When I look back, she's gone.

I hitch up my skirt so I can run. This is definitely the hill that leads up to Crown Street, where Aunt Rachel's shop is. On either side of the street there are barefoot kids hanging out. Front doors are wide open, the pavements are cracked; it's dusty and hot. A little girl catches my eye and I gasp, feeling as if she's seen the real me inside this stranger.

Running turns out to be impossible. This body and these clothes are weighing me down and I'm still clutching the carpetbag. I slow down and think back to how I'd shattered the hairbrush.

Nightie-girl had said something like 'Is this about the race, Fan?' But she didn't make me answer. I'm sorry about the brush but I couldn't help it, I was terrified.

Still am.

Finally I'm here, on Crown Street, so close to where Aunt Rachel's shop should be. I turn left and keep going, trying to see what's different and what's the same. Nothing's the same! I've walked too far now, so I go back over old ground.

I keep pacing, looking up to where I think our place is meant to stand.

This is the right building. But the sign reads *Ernest Ireland, Pastry Cook*. Through the window I can see pies and buns on dark wooden shelves. I press my head to the glass and try to stop myself from crying. *Wake up, Cat.* This can't be happening.

As I pull back I catch my reflection. So that's what I look like. Older, maybe sixteen, with curves in places where my own body has none. This girl has a long face, masses of hair. Looking into her dark eyes is terrifying, at first, but they sparkle as if she's a fun person to be around. Somehow they make me feel calmer. *But why am I you?*

A bell startles me—the shop door opens and a woman comes out. She wipes her hands on her white apron.

'You all right, dearie?'

I'm not all right, but she's a stranger and she'll think I'm lying or mad if I tell her anything. I shake my head and go back the way I came.

The only familiar thing is the sky. I look up, wishing hard that I could see Mum's flight coming in to land. But there's nothing but clouds. If I'm really in the past, my family doesn't exist. I don't either. I crumble into more tears and keep walking without knowing where to go or who to ask for help. I am lost in a way that I can't explain to anyone.

10

School

I'm standing on the corner of Beach Road. I've crossed here hundreds of times, but I stare at the buildings that line the street. What is this place? There is nothing I know. Nothing familiar except the street names. Where is the bakery that Ma lets us buy buns from on occasion? Where are the carts? The horses? And what are the people wearing? They're dressed in less than their undergarments. In the street!

On both sides of the street are shops, only not shops like those I know. They have colourful windows with signs that I don't understand. One says *Cheap Phones* and I look in the window at the display of boxes and small black objects. What are they? I've heard of telephones but they are large impressive things on the wall—nothing like this.

Another shop is selling liquor, and I watch a woman walk out with a bag of clinking bottles, and she's talking to herself. But she's not like those in the pub that sit too long and drink too many pints, those that Da has to boot out with his broom at the end of the night.

People are eating outside, sitting at tables under umbrellas, and I take my eyes away from their skimpy clothes. But not fast enough. I spy a man older than Da wearing no shirt, with muscles like he swims, and with dark glasses on his face.

I spin around, looking for something I know. I see a shop with boards that look like the ones the lifesavers use down at Coogee. But these boards are short and colourful, and a girl is inspecting them like she plans to buy one, but surely not. No girls surf on boards in my time.

There's a loud roaring sound overhead and I stare up into the sky, not knowing what I'll find. A white bird-like thing passes across the sky. What strange flying machine is this?

But this isn't my time. This is some strange time. I think of what the lady said at the baths. That Mina died in 1984. She would have been ninety-three years old. That's positively ancient. So, this is the future. And it's not like anything I've ever imagined. At least I'm still in Coogee. Not my Coogee, but it is Coogee.

Two people bump into me, so engrossed in each other, they don't notice the short me in a school uniform with the racing heart and the fear.

I hear the rumbling of a horse and cart and look up for the familiar sight, but there's just a boy with a strange backwards hat on and pants hanging too low, rolling towards me on a plank of wood with tiny wheels. He speeds past and leaps off his plank, kicking the back so it flies up and he catches it and keeps walking. If I wasn't so out of sorts then I might like to have a go at that.

Sleek, enclosed cars are speeding furiously down the road, jostling like horses in a race. I'm not sure how to cross. Perhaps I cannot. But if I'm to get to Victoria Grammar then I must.

I step gingerly out onto the road and am met with a loud, angry blasting sound. I leap back to the gutter just in time as a red car speeds past. My heart is galloping. What if I'm stuck on this corner forever?

Then a woman about my sister Kath's age wearing very tight, bright clothes appears, running on the spot. Maybe she can help me.

'Excuse me,' I say.

But she doesn't look at me. Can she not hear me?

'Excuse me?' I say, in my loudest voice, which Ma would tick me off for if she heard it.

But still the woman faces straight ahead and doesn't answer. And then I notice she has a little white stick hanging from her ear. What could it be that prevents her from hearing my voice? I'd like to ask her, but she runs across the road finding a small break in cars.

I run after her, trying to be ladylike, and then not caring, as long as I make it to the other side without being squashed.

Safe, I breathe for a second, but then a man starts yelling at me, or maybe not at me. He seems to be talking to himself shouting loudly, like he's arguing with a ghost perhaps.

I hurry on, passing more shops with windows like I've never seen. I weave through people sitting at tables outside on the footpath with food in front of them. Imagine eating outside in public like this. It's like picnicking on a table not a beach.

My stomach swirls. I didn't even eat breakfast this morning. I stare at the food. Then up to the person eating it. They look like a man, but they have very long fair hair and bright red colour on their lips. They lift something dripping towards their mouth and take a large bite and I look away quickly, not wanting to be rude.

I hurry away towards Victoria College. I only know where it is because I've passed it on my way to train at Wylie's Baths. Even Mina is impressed by its fine buildings.

I stop outside the large iron gates. I can't imagine ever belonging at a school like this, but here I am, dressed the same as the other girls heading inside. It's been a long time since I've been to school. I stopped years ago to help Da in the pub and Ma in the kitchen, and swim in between.

'Cat!' Someone is yelling.

I look down for a lost cat.

'Cat!'

Turning around I see a girl running towards me with a paper bag in her hand. Am I supposed to know her?

'Feeling better now, Cat?' the girl asks me.

Cat? I'm a cat?

'Do you know what's happening to me?' I say, turning to her and hoping she can help me.

'What? You just wanted to get out of training, didn't you?'

'Training?' What is she talking about?

'Why do you keep answering my questions with a question? Yes, training. You know that thing we are supposed to do every morning in the pool!' She starts to walk off and I hurry after her. She clearly knows who I am.

'Excuse me, but can you help me. I'm not Cat. Something strange is happening…' I start to say.

She turns around and gives me a worried-Ma sort of look. 'Are you hungry? Did you miss breakfast? Here, take these. Don't tell Dad. I don't think Tiny Teddies and Barbecue Shapes are exactly on the swimming diet!'

She shoves two small things into my hands. So this new me is a swimmer. That news makes me slightly cheered. And my name must be Cat. Behind us a bell sounds and everyone starts to hurry past.

'I have to get to class,' says the girl I'm supposed to know. 'Wait for me tonight right here and we'll get the bus home together. Or Dad will go nuts! He hates it when you go without me!'

Happy to be finally told what to do, I nod at her. It seems we're sisters. I want to ask her what Dad *going nuts* is? Why can't she just say what she means? Then I realise it doesn't matter about the nuts, it just matters that I have a new Dad. But I don't want one, I want my own, my Da.

And then an even more worrying thought worms its way into my head. If I'm this Cat person, what has happened to her? Is it possible that she's me? Have we somehow changed bodies? Swapped times? Is she stuck too, right now, being me?

Another bell sounds and I follow the other girls. Two girls hurry past me. One has the darkest skin I've ever seen. The children at the school I went to were all white. This is wonderfully different.

At least I know my name now. Cat! I do a little *meow* just to keep my spirits up, and head down the hall. And stop. At the sight of hundreds of girls, chattering, laughing and eating! Not just bread either, but fruit and unrecognisable things. Then I remember the girl, my sister, shoved something at me—two little colourful packages. I hold one of them and shake it near my ear and can hear something inside. I tug at the top, and it rips apart, exploding little shapes all over the ground. Too hungry to care, I scoop them up and try one. It is salty and so delicious, and I shove them all in my mouth.

I take out the other little bag. This time I open it carefully and dive in. These are the sweetest little biscuits shaped like teddy bears. How are they all carved so perfectly when they're so small? They are almost too lovely for eating. I nibble an ear. They're better than Ma's best Sunday cake. And no mixing, no rolling or cutting the dough by hand, just open the bag and there they are. What magic is this?

I imagine Dewey's delighted face if she could see these little bears. Dearest Dewey. What if she's still looking for me at Wylie's Baths? I blink away the thought of my sister.

Before I can lose myself in worries, I feel a jab in the ribs. I spin around ready to fight, my fists up the way brother Con is teaching me, which annoys Ma because it's so unladylike. I must be feeling very jumpy to put my fists up so quickly.

'Whoa! You're punchy this morning, Cat!'

A short girl with wild black hair, even messier than my real hair is when I haven't brushed it, is grinning at me.

'Come on, Cat. We have English,' she says, linking her arm through mine and pulling me with her against the tide of girls. I don't know who this girl is but I decide to let her sweep me away.

'Do I like English?' I risk a strange question hoping she'll think it's funny.

She pulls a face that suggests she's used to my funny questions. 'Not particularly, but then you don't like much. Except swimming, and then I'm not even sure you always like that,' she says, sounding slightly puzzled.

'You're wrong. I love swimming,' I tell her.

'Really? That's good, you seemed a bit confused the other day,' she tells me.

Oh. No. Not only have I swapped times. And bodies, but I don't like swimming either. What is this punishment?

'Did you remember my copy of the play?'

'Play?'

'Cat! I texted you this morning.'

I wish I understood what she was talking about. She seems so disappointed.

'Bring it with you tomorrow! Promise?'

I nod, and she tucks her hair behind her ear trying to contain it. 'Come on! Ms Bennett will not be happy if we're late.'

'What date is it?' I ask the girl.

'Twenty-fourth,' she tells me.

How can I ask her what year it is without her guessing that something's up? I try a smile so that the girl will think I'm being funny and risk trying a playful game. 'Correct, but I bet you don't know the month and the year!'

She laughs and looks at me. 'Honestly, Cat sometimes I worry about you! It's March, 2021.'

Oh. I feel a little faint. I reach out for the wall and lean my hand against it. How is this possible? How have I found myself all the way into the twenty-first century?

'Cat?'

I'm too busy trying to breathe to speak. My new friend squeezes my arm even tighter and drags me off down the hall.

She pushes the door open and we tumble in. Everyone else is seated and they turn to stare at us.

'Girls?' A teacher with long red hair pulled into a low ponytail looks at us from the front of the room. 'I'm Ms Jackson, your CRT,' she says.

Ms Jackson? What's a Ms? What's a CRT? Does it mean something?

'Apologies for our tardiness, it is all my fault,' I say most politely, wondering what punishments for lateness exist in this time.

The teacher blinks for a second and my hands sweat at the thought of the strap being whipped across them. It never happened to me at school, but my brother Con got the strap once.

Then she smiles at me and her smile is light and sweet. 'Apology accepted,' she says. 'Your names?'

'She's Catherine and I'm Lucy,' says my new friend.

Now I know my new friend's name. Lucy. I like the sound of that. It's a little like Dewey.

'Catherine, Lucy, please take a seat. We're talking about *Romeo and Juliet*,' says the teacher.

Unsure of what just happened I sit down at one of the two tables at the front. I'm aware of girls watching me, and of Lucy looking at me strangely too.

'We're discussing the themes of fate and free will. Has anyone got something to add?' the teacher asks.

Various hands spring up and girls start talking. My school was all needlework and cursive writing, not talking about themes. I don't even know what themes are. I listen as hard as I can to what the students are saying. I've never been in a room of people who offer their thoughts up for discussion. Even my boisterous family defers to Ma on most things. It's almost thrilling watching the classroom of girls getting agitated and outspoken. I wish I could contribute something.

'Obviously they were always destined to die. It was fated in the stars,' says a girl behind me.

'Yes, it's all about fate!' says another.

The teacher looks at Lucy and me. 'Catherine, what do you think?'

I blink several times. I don't feel ready to speak up. Lucy nods at me, encouraging me to say something.

'Fate doesn't exist,' I say. 'If it did then it wouldn't matter how much we tried at something.' I'm slightly giddy as the words come out of my mouth. I don't know if what I say makes sense but when I swim, I know there's no fate in winning or losing. It's all about hard work.

As the discussion swirls around me, I see Lucy frowning at me. Perhaps this Cat person doesn't speak up in class. Perhaps she's quiet and without opinions. Perhaps I'm completely out of my depth.

'Now your teacher left you some work to do on the theme of fate, so take out your laptops and make a start,' says the teacher.

All around me girls start opening up silver contraptions. I look over at Lucy. Even she is opening something and there's a pinging noise and colour and light pour out of the thing in front of her. Lucy starts pressing the little black keys and there is a flash and pictures light up on the thing.

Terrified I leap up, causing my chair to tumble behind me, and I run out of the room.

11

Pub

I sit on a fat stone step in a quiet laneway, with my back against a door. I hope it doesn't open suddenly.

What else is in this bag? Maybe some clues. The thin towel I used is still heavy and wet. There's an ugly sort of shower cap. By digging down I find a purse. Inside there are some big brown coins with a man's head on one side and a dragon and knight on the other. EDWARDVS VII, REX—I know that word: *rex* means king!

But that's no help at all.

I keep going over what's happened, then loop to the beginning and see it all again. I'm stuck in this moment, scared of what to do next.

Hours pass. The light in the sky has changed and I don't want to be alone here after dark. The only thing that makes sense is to go back to where I left nightie-girl. I get up and brush the dust off my skirt, turn off

Crown Street and walk down the hill.

'Miss! Please, Miss!' a scruffy boy tugs hard on my sleeve. 'My sister, Miss. She's hurt.' He's got a dirty face and bare feet. I guess he's around my real age. I try to keep my feet planted as he pulls me.

'I can't help you. Let go!' I snatch my arm away.

'She's bleeding, Miss!'

I look for an adult, but then I realise that I must look like the closest thing to this boy—he doesn't know I'm only thirteen inside. So I follow him towards a side street. Sticking out from behind a wall is a thin white leg. I drop the bag on the cobblestones and run to the little girl. She's in a filthy grey dress, and curled over so I can't see her face. There's a pool of something dark on the stones.

'I'll get help,' I say, touching her arm.

She moans.

'Have you got a phone?' I ask the boy, 'Oh no, is there such thing as phones?'

The boy frowns at me.

'*Telephones*,' I say, louder. 'Ambulance? Er, hospital?' He grabs my sleeve again and points frantically up Crown Street, so I struggle to my feet in the long skirt and run in that direction.

When I reach the top of the hill I turn back for a moment and realise something's not right. The girl is on her feet and she's got my bag. Now the two of them are sprinting down the hill—it was a trick, she wasn't hurt at all!

'Stop!' I yell. I hitch up my skirt and chase after them. 'My bag!'

I'll never catch up.

The girl looks behind her and as she turns back she collides with a man coming down the steps of his house. She screams and the boy yells, yanking her out of the man's grip. I come hurtling towards them as the bag flies into the air and the thieves keep running. The bag lands at my feet but I can't stop in time—I trip over it and land with a smack.

As the pain shoots up my arms, my head is dark and spinning like I've been rattled hard. It's like the way I felt in the water—maybe this time trap or bad dream is wearing off! But as I blink I can still see the boy and girl far away. A hand reaches down to me. At first I try to get up by myself but this outfit is like a cocoon. I grip the hand and I'm lifted to my feet in one strong pull.

'Thank you,' I say, still breathless.

He tilts his cap. He's a tall, Asian teenager with black hair and dark eyes. He's holding a book against his chest: *Verses, Popular and Humorous* by Henry Lawson. We've got a Henry Lawson book at home. The thought of that and the sting in my arms and the throbbing in my head finally beats me—I cry right there in front of him.

'Are you very hurt, Fanny? Please don't cry.'

'I'm fine,' I blub, definitely not fine at all, and wishing I could shout *My name is Cat* for the whole world to hear. He offers me a handkerchief, but I'm not wiping a stranger's germs on my face. Even if it's not really my face. I take it though. 'You called me Fanny. Do you know me?' I sniff and wipe my face on my sleeve.

He blinks and then laughs. 'Very funny. Con's always saying you could have been on the stage.'

I suppose I could ask who Con is but he'll only think I'm joking again. He gestures down the hill so I decide I might as well walk with him. We go over what happened—the girl smashing into him, the screaming and yelling, me flying over the bag.

He says, 'You were *fast*. I didn't know girls could run like that.'

'Girls can do anything,' I snap.

He doesn't argue, luckily. Then he says, 'Speaking of fast, I hear you're an outstanding swimmer.'

I smile a little. At least that's one true thing.

'I wish you'd teach me sometime, Fan. I could pay, you know. I've never even been in the water.'

'Why not?'

'Caught up with my studies, and scared too, if I'm honest. Far as I get is standing on the cliffs.' He holds his book out in front of us. *'Friends may be gone in the morning fair, but the cliffs by the ocean are always there, lovers may leave when the wind is chill, but the cliffs by the ocean are steadfast still.* Do you enjoy poetry, Fanny?'

'Uh, sure.'

'Excellent. What is your favourite poem?'

'Let me think…'

Why did I say I like poetry? I don't know a single poem. The only thing that comes into my head is the slam poem Lucy and I made up for English. It was called Scholarship Girl. 'Okay…well'—I clear my throat—*'There is no let-up, not from the moment we get-up, if you're this good you have to stay that way, never let it get away, scholarship girl.'*

The boy looks stunned but he smiles politely, and I can't help giggling. I wish I could tell Lucy. I think she'd like him. He's a bit proper and I hope he doesn't keep quoting Henry Lawson poems, but this is the first time all day that I haven't felt terrified.

'This is where I leave you, unfortunately,' he says.

Maybe he could help me in some way but I don't have the guts to ask. We're outside the hotel, the place that I'm supposed to call home.

'Give my regards to Con, won't you?' he says.

'Sure. What was your name again?'

He looks upset. 'Arthur Gon,' he replies before he twists on the balls of his feet and walks away quickly. There's no way for me to explain why I had to ask. I'm still holding his handkerchief but he's already across the busy street and I'm not stepping in front of a moving horse for him.

I can't worry about Arthur's feelings now. The sun is going down. Mum, Dad and Maisy are so far away that the worry is like knives in my stomach. It's time to go inside.

This isn't like any hotel I've been in. It's a pub bar, jam-packed and loud with crowds of men in shabby jackets and flat caps, no tables or chairs, and sawdust all over the floor. It smells like a stable and sounds like a street riot.

'There you are, Fan!' yells a deep voice from behind the bar. As petrified as I am, I try to make my way over there but I'm trapped in a huddle of men with missing teeth and red faces. I hate the way they're looking at me, but then I remember that I'm taller and stronger in this body.

'Excuse me!' I say and I ram my way through, sending a few men stumbling backwards.

'Blimey, who's she think she is?' slurs one.

'She's Tommy Durack's favourite daughter. That'll be your last drink in here if you're not careful!'

If *she*'s his favourite, I wonder if Tommy Durack will realise that I'm not actually her. What'll he do if he does? I need to pretend I'm her now more than ever.

At the bar I find a man who looks as old as my grandpa.

'Where've you been all day? You've got a face like a pickled egg.' He has an Irish accent, of course.

'Uh, sorry...Father.'

The man barks a short laugh that makes me jump.

'*Father*? What's happened to Da?'

'Sorry! I mean Da.'

Luckily he's too distracted to notice how much I'm shaking. He pours beer and glances at me. 'You've got a funny look about you. Hey!' he yells down the bar, 'Look at your sister, Con. She look funny to you?'

So that's Con, Arthur's friend. A teenage boy peers through a fringe the colour of shiny copper as he pulls on a beer tap.

'No funnier than usual, Da,' he yells back and they both laugh but not in a mean way. They really believe I'm her.

I watch Tommy Durack hand drink after drink to the men. He takes their money—the same big brown coins I found in the purse—and talks to them in a serious, gravelly voice. He looks at me and winks. Behind him, pinned all along the wall, are newspaper cuttings—it's hard to see from here but I can make out the words LADIES SWIMMING RACE.

'Go on upstairs, darlin'.'

'Okay,' I reply. Then I panic in case *okay* hasn't been invented yet, but he doesn't react so I head towards some wooden stairs.

I come to a dingy hallway: floorboards covered with a worn-out carpet runner. There's a musty, gassy smell but it's also hot and stuffy. Up here the noise from the bar is muffled. There's a pendant light but it's so dim it might as well be a candle. I can hear clanging pots in one of the rooms off the hallway.

A woman pokes her head out of the room. 'There you are!' she says, crossly. 'We were about to send out a search party. Where on earth have you been? As if I didn't know. Help me with the tea, right this minute, everyone else has their hands full.'

My heart's thumping. This must be Fan's mother.

The room is a kitchen. It has a long table in the middle with a bench on each side. The woman shoves a poker in the door of a cast-iron oven to move some hot coals around. Saucepans and cooking utensils that look like instruments of torture hang on the wall, and in the corner there's a bench covered in a pale-green embroidered cloth. My eyes are drawn down the cloth to where there's something sticking out.

A tail!

'*Aaarrrgghhh!*'

'What in heavens?' The woman spins round with the poker.

I jab my finger at the corner of the room.

'Oh grand, got one did we?' she says cheerfully. 'Don't stand there all day, Fan, get rid of it down the back stairs.' She uses her foot to kick the thing out from under the cloth. It's a huge dead rat in a trap. Its eyes are open and there's blood everywhere. I've had enough of blood today; I'm almost a vegetarian!

A boy bursts in, dark hair sticking out in all directions.

'Fan looks strange, Ma.' He peers up at me with big hazel eyes and licks off a milk moustache.

'There's a rat in the trap, Frankie,' says the woman. 'Be a good lad and deal with it. Fanny, stir this while I make the rest of our tea.'

She hands me a wooden spoon from a huge pot and turns to the table to knead some dough. I thought she meant tea as in a cup of tea, but she means dinner. I stir carefully, trying to look like I know what I'm doing. I'm a terrible cook but this beats picking up a dead animal.

To my right there's a jug with a gauzy cloth over it weighted down with beads. Flies are buzzing around the top. There's a sudden sourness up my nose. I think it's off milk!

'Lucky I was here to save you,' says the boy, Frankie, dangling the rat by the tail.

'Because I'm a girl?' I snap.

'No, Fan, cos you're squeamish.' He heads down a stairwell, flashing me a smile.

Behind me, Fanny's mum starts chattering fast. 'Tough as old boots is our Fan. Right, my girl, it's wash day tomorrow so I've a job and a half getting the food done because, as I don't have to tell you, we won't be able to stop to scratch our backsides. Now then, did you remember to thank Mr Wylie for all his encouragement, Fan, because I won't have anyone thinking the Duracks don't have manners.' Her voice goes up and down like piano scales.

'Yes, Ma,' I say quietly.

'I'm sorry you didn't win your race yesterday, Fan. Truly. It's a blow for you, I know. Is it really the sort of thing a young woman in your position should be doing? Well, I don't know, daughter, to tell you the truth of the matter...'

She goes on like this for a long time. The gist is that Fanny shouldn't be devoting time to swimming when there's more important stuff to be done. I don't know what that stuff is yet. School? A job? I still don't even know how old I'm supposed to be. This is a lonely and terrifying trap to be in, whatever it is. Not even Fanny's mum suspects that something completely wild has happened to her own kid. I picture my own mum and almost start crying again, but I can't wimp out.

Ma stops kneading and yells out the doorway. 'Dewey Durack! Get your backside in here, girl!'

Dewey! That's her name. I knew it was *something-ooey*! When I hear her footsteps I turn around, the spoon dripping stew on the floor, and smile at her for the first time. She smiles back, luckily, even after the way I treated her earlier. I feel relieved to see her. She was there when this thing happened. That has to mean something. I need to find out exactly what she saw at Wylie's Baths this morning.

12

New Home

My day has confounded me. After fleeing the classroom I sat on the dusty floor of the corridor and choked back tears. I am not a crier. Sarah Fanny Durack does not cry. Not when I lose in the pool. Not when my toenail peels off with infection. Not when I had measles. I don't cry. But today I nearly did.

Lucy found me. She told me it didn't matter if I'd left my laptop home because I could work with her. I have no idea what a laptop even is, but I couldn't tell her that. Lucy is almost as sweet as Dewey.

Everyone stared when I came back in, but I pretended I was fine. I'm good at acting. I won prizes for cakewalking before swimming took over, but that was just funny faces and clowning around.

I didn't let Lucy out of my sight after that. She's very smart and knows things that even my older brother wouldn't and he's the smartest person I know. She shared her lunch with me. It came in a series of metal tins each filled with different foods like tiny red tomatoes that popped seeds into my mouth when I bit them and salty crackers covered in cheese, and I had trouble stopping myself from finishing both hers and mine.

Now I'm sitting next to my sister, whose name I think is Maisy because it's written on the tag on her satchel. We're on the bus, which is nothing like the trams I'm used to. It keeps stopping suddenly and it's jerky and crowded and the seats are covered in soft padded fabric. Maisy has little white things stuck in her ears like the woman I saw in the street. They seem to be making noise and she's ignoring me.

I need to talk to Maisy because she might have answers for me. Without thinking, I reach across and yank the white string connecting to the thing in Maisy's right ear. She yelps and glares at me.

'Cat!'

'Sorry. I just want to talk.'

'I'm listening to music,' she says sharply.

I think of how keen Dewey is to talk to me, and how often we lie in bed whispering late into the night. But then Maisy reaches over and pushes the thing into my ear and I hear singing that's sweet and gentle and female. Maisy smiles at me, and I take it as an apology of sorts and I lean closer, listening to the melody. I've never heard a song like this. And it's going straight into my head.

'How is this possible?' I say.

Maisy shushes me. 'Too loud, Cat,' she says.

'What?'

She touches the small flat rectangle thing in her hand that I think is a 'cheap phone', and the music stops. 'You're yelling. Just talk quietly,' she says.

'Oh. Sorry,' I reply with a smile, wanting to know what the magical thing is and how it glows with light like the flame of a candle. But I can't think of a way to ask.

She rolls her eyes at me, but it's warm, and I think that maybe I'm growing on her.

'Can we listen to the song now?' she says, and music swims into my ear. The girl is singing about love. It's like poetry but all running together. She's hurting because he's left her. The words are silly, but still my eyes fill with tears for this poor girl. Or maybe not for her. Maybe for me. Because I'm in this bewildering place and I don't know how I'll ever get home. I sniff loudly and wipe my nose with my hand.

Maisy looks across and frowns at me. 'Are you crying, Cat?'

'Just something in my eye,' I say quickly.

Outside I see a church I recognise—the Proddy

church, not our Catholic one. It's not far from the pub. I yank the white thing from my ear and leap up, ready to alight at the next stop.

'What are you doing, Cat?'

'I've just seen something. I need to get off.'

'But we're ages from home,' she says.

'Please,' I say, in the voice that always wins Dewey over. It doesn't quite sound the same in Cat's voice, but it seems to work.

Maisy sighs and reaches for her bag. I don't wait for her. I start hurrying down the bus, pushing past people. How do I make it stop? The bus takes a corner and I'm flung to the side, bashing into a man who glares an angry face at me.

I hear a ding. Like magic, the bus pulls in to the side of the road and I throw myself towards the doors, waiting for them to open. I hear a woman tutting at me like I'm badly behaved, but I don't care. I need to find the pub.

Finally the doors open and I leap out onto the street. I try to work out my bearings. I think the pub is right.

Maisy hurries behind me. 'What are you doing, Cat?'

But I'm not up for conversation. She can either keep up or go home. I set off as fast as I can with these little legs. We pass a shop that seems to have displays of clothes for dogs. That can't be right. But this shop is called *Your Canine Friend.* The longer I'm here in this odd future, the more confused I feel.

We reach the end of the road and I look down the hill. I skipped across this street so many times on the way home from the baths, running late for dinner, or chores. My heart is starting to beat faster, like it does just before a race. I hope the pub is the same. That it's my way back.

Hurrying now I hear Maisy yell behind me. 'You jaywalked!' She catches up with me. 'You'll get run over!'

Ignoring her, I keep walking towards the flower shop with its buckets of roses and carnations on display.

I see the pub. But it's not right. There are bright lights and ugly signs and the front is all slick and painted black. I rush to the door, desperate to go in, hoping to find my family, even if they have been scrubbed clean too.

I make it up the steps. Maisy is yelling at me, but I push open the heavy door. Inside, there's no rowdy scene, just awful screaming music. My shoes are sticky on the black carpet. There are rows of people sitting on stools staring at big boxes like cupboards that whir and light up. What is this place?

'You can't be in here, love!' a man calls from behind the bar.

I look for something familiar, but it's all gone.

'You can't be here!' He shouts this time.

And I turn and flee, storming straight past Maisy.

'*Ca-at!*' she yells.

I don't stop. My family have vanished. There's no evidence we ever existed. This place is ugly, and I want to go home.

'Wait!' Maisy grabs my arm and I pull away.

'I want to go home!' I tell her, knowing there is no way she can understand.

'Do you think I want to be here? It smells,' she says angrily.

'Well I hate it more than you do!' I yell.

'Everything's a competition with you, Cat!' She sounds really upset and it makes me stop my stormy walk and pull her into a hug. It's not her fault.

'Whoa! What was that for, Cat?'

'Nothing. Let's just go. This was a mistake,' I tell her.

'Yeah, I'll say!' she replies.

We walk down the street that I used to know so well. I'm trying to keep myself together while Maisy talks nonstop, distracting me. Mostly she's going on about swimming and pathways and how happy it makes her dad when she begs to do extra training, and I wish I could tell her how lucky she is that her dad can watch her train when my Da never saw me swim.

'Dad's probably wondering where we are,' says

Maisy as she stops outside a shop. I realise this is where she lives. Where *I* live.

I'm about to meet the man I hope will only be my temporary father. The thought makes me miss Da more than ever. Maisy disappears in through a door. It has a sign that says 'Mini-Mart'. I follow her, patting down my hair and smoothing my skirt to prepare for my new family.

Inside I gape at the walls. At the colour and the clutter. At the shelves jammed full of packets and bottles and cans. At labels I try to read. The shop is dark and quiet. In fact there is no one here except a man with very short cropped hair and a brightly coloured shirt with flowers on it standing behind the counter with a newspaper open in front of him. He's smiling, and he looks like a...father.

'Hello, girls. Good day?'

What to call him? 'Yes thank you, father.'

He smiles and his eyes crinkle at the corners. 'Father? That's a bit formal, Cat!'

'Sorry, Da!'

This time he laughs and the sound is catchy. 'What's wrong with "Dad"?'

I smile at him, and my glance drifts down to the display cabinet under the counter. There are boxes and boxes of what I think are sweets twinkling at me.

'Father, do you have a bull's eye? Or a brandy ball?'

He laughs. 'No, we have milk bottles, pineapples and raspberries. Jelly babies and snakes. You know all this, Cat.'

'Oh, may I try some?'

'I suppose you can have a couple, but only if you stop calling me *Father*!'

He drops some brightly coloured sweets into my hand and they're soft and squishy, not hard like the boiled ones we have on special days. I pop the yellow one in my mouth.

'Delicious,' I tell him. I cannot believe I live in a place where there are so many sweets. Dewey would simply melt at the thought.

'You hate them!' Maisy says stepping closer. 'Gelatine! Remember!'

I have no idea what she's talking about. Cat is obviously a person with no taste.

Maisy sighs like I'm being difficult. I look at all the packets of food. Ma would be beside herself. I've heard of food in cans, but never have we had anything like that. I pick up a blue can with little beans on the front— 'Baked Beans'. I wonder what they taste like. There's another called tuna and something labelled spaghetti with a picture of what looks like worms. I'm not sure I want to try that.

'Are you hungry, Cat?'

The father is holding something round out to me. I take it and it's warm in my hand. I bite the edge. It's salty and crisp.

'Try this, Maisy!'

'I never eat potato scallops. You know that.'

So that's what it's called. This treat made of potato. It's like Ma's fried potato only so much better. I'll have to learn the secrets, so I can show her. Somehow, I will find a way back. I have to. The thought of never seeing my family again is too hard to bear.

'Can I please have another?' I ask.

'Go and make a smoothie or something healthy,' says Father.

Obviously the potato scallops are precious and I can only have one. How very disappointing. Maisy opens a door and I see the staircase leading up. It's not so different from the pub. I follow my new sister to my new home, still eating the salty scallop, and wondering what new world I am in.

Maisy drops her bag down on the chair and tosses her music device on the bench before slouching into the kitchen and opening a shiny metal door. She leans in and sighs.

'If I make the smoothie can you pack the dishwasher?' she says.

I don't know what a smoothie is, but I make a guess about the rest. 'Do you mean I have to wash up?'

Maisy peers around the metal door and looks at me. 'Yep! There's only almond milk. Is that okay?'

Almond milk? How do you milk an almond? I'm not going to risk asking, so instead I pick up the box she's placed in front of me.

'It's cold!'

'Yeah. It was in the fridge! Cat, why are you being so strange?' Maisy turns away and opens the top of the metal door. A rush of steam pours out, like something magic. I come up close behind Maisy, who is foraging inside. I lean over and reach out. My fingers are met with icy coldness of the 'steam'. How do they keep cold in?

'Here they are!' Maisy tosses a bag onto the bench. It says raspberries. I'm in the way and she looks cross, like Ma does when I stand in the kitchen in winter with my back to the stove.

'Can you grab the bullet?' Maisy says.

'Bullet?'

'Are you okay, Cat?'

I nod, pulling a funny face like I would with Dewey. Maisy smiles. 'Go and sit down!' she says.

But I can't. All around me are machines. I can't stop looking. A loud whirring noise startles me and I spin around to see Maisy shaking something vigorously.

'What are you doing?' I yell.

She stops shaking and unscrews the end. I watch her pour thick pink milk into two glasses. She hands me one.

'Thank you,' I say, taking a sip from the glass. It's freezing cold and sweet and it's the best thing I've ever tasted. 'It's delicious,' I say.

I take a big slurp this time and my head freezes on the inside. I pull a face with the pain of it.

'Ice-cream headache! Hit your head like Dad does,' Maisy tells me.

I bash the side of my head with my fist and she giggles. 'Not like that, silly! Like this,' she says. She taps the front of my forehead with her fingers. 'Drink slower, Cat! I'm going to do homework. You're even stranger than usual!'

After Maisy goes, I open the top part of fridge again, and the steam swirls cold around me. If I'm stuck in this future for a little while I may as well try to learn something about it.

13
Tea

At dinner there are ten of us at the kitchen table. It's gloomy up here now the sun's gone down and I wish I knew what that gassy smell is, or maybe it's better I don't. There's another floor above that Ma called 'the guest beds' so that's how this is a hotel. But it's not posh. I think the Duracks are scraping by. It looks like a lot of hard work, even more than my dad spending all hours in the shop and my mum serving passengers in the sky.

We're squashed together on long benches. The conversation is loud and overlapping so it's hard to think straight. A man called John, who is Fan's eldest brother, had a newspaper earlier and I checked the date: it's 1908. When I saw that I felt like I'd taken a solo trip to the moon. How am I ever going to get home?

I've worked out that Fan is the sixth child out of nine. No wonder Ma looks tired. Most of them are at the table, but they've mentioned someone called Thomas Junior who's 'on the road', whatever that means. John looks like my maths teacher, cranky in a brown suit. Opposite me are Kathleen and Mary, both pretty and neat in long skirts and pinned-up brown hair. Then there's Con, the barman with the nice arms, and Mick, who could be about twelve, and then little Frankie, the rat boy. And Dewey, who is sitting next to me, her arm pressed into mine. I'm bursting to tell her that I'm really Cat, and I'm thirteen, the same as her. I know her age because Ma told her off before dinner for 'forgetting to put the dripping in the meat safe last night' and said Dewey should know better at thirteen. The meat safe looks like a small rabbit hutch and it's got cut-up bits of cow in it. It doesn't feel cold like a fridge so I can't believe this whole family hasn't died of food poisoning.

'You're awful solemn tonight, Fan,' says Mr Durack.

'Oh, um, just tired, Mister—er, *Da*.'

'Mister Da!' laughs grubby little Mick down the other end of the table. 'Fan's cuckoo!'

'Hush there, Mick,' says Da, gruffly, and to me he says, 'You'll come first next race, I can feel it.'

'Or she won't,' says Ma.

'What d'ya mean, woman?'

'All I'm saying, Tommy, is Fan's given it a fair crack and if it's not to be it's not to be. I need her here, not gallivanting to Mr Wylie's baths every five minutes. And as for the money to enter a race, well, honestly, we've got mouths to feed.'

'Stop yarning. My customers were only too happy to put their hands in their pockets for our Fan to go to the swimming carnivals this season.'

'Ha! They're so drunk they don't know what they're doing half the time.'

'Those men'd go down there and watch our girl swim every Saturday if they were allowed.'

'I'll bet they would,' mutters Kathleen.

'Out of the question,' says John, sternly. 'No men at ladies carnivals and that's how it should stay.' He seems like the grouch of the family.

Kathleen and Mary roll their eyes at each other, and then they smile at me.

It seems extreme that men aren't allowed to go to swimming carnivals, but I'm too scared to say a word. Maybe coming here was a mistake, because all I'm thinking about is what they'll do if they realise I'm not Fanny. I picture all ten of them crowding around, shoving me, shouting in their Irish voices: *What have you done with Fan?*

'If Fanny isn't eating her stew, can I have it?' says Frankie.

'Course she's eating it, it's her favourite,' says Ma.

But I'm just moving it around the plate because I don't have the guts to say I'm vegetarian. The hunks of potatoes and carrots are floating in brown juice with stringy bits of meat. Last year I swore I'd never eat meat for as long as I lived. But now I'm so hungry I might faint. If I eat meat a hundred years before I was even born, does that count? Food might help me think straight.

Da's chair scrapes on the wooden floor. 'Come on, Con, best get back downstairs to the mob.'

Con reaches over to my plate, stabs a potato and shoves it in his mouth. He winks at me before he follows his dad.

'Not like you letting him get away with that, Fan,' says Kathleen.

I laugh nervously, wanting to say 'That's because I'm *not* Fan!' But I've dodged suspicion again—they're already onto the next topic of conversation. I spear a piece of soft carrot, dripping in meaty juice and silently apologise to cows before I put it in my mouth.

After tea, the chores keep coming for hours and hours. All I can do is follow the other girls but I'm always a step behind.

Dewey and I are sent downstairs to sweep the sawdust from the floor of the pub while Da and Con close up. It's revolting. I'd rather muck out a stable because at least horses deserve it. And I'm so tired—the only thing holding me up is this broom but now is my chance to ask questions. I need to sound casual.

'So, Dewey, we had a good time at Wylie's today. Didn't we?'

'I'm sure I did, Fan. But you stayed in the water awful long and when you got out it was as if you'd had a dose of something.'

'Were you watching me the whole time I was swimming?'

'Of course I was. Don't nag at me, you sound like Ma.'

'I'm not nagging, it's just—you didn't see anything strange? In the water?'

'I don't know what you're asking me.'

'Well, okay, how come you didn't want to swim too?'

'How come I…Fan, are you angry because I didn't train with you? But what good would I be?'

Dewey's getting upset. This is going terribly.

'I didn't mean anything bad.'

'You said you wanted me to time you, and time you I did.' Her voice sounds like a squeaky wheel. 'And now you're saying I should have somehow kept time and swum against you at the same time!'

How do I turn this around?

At that moment Da walks across the wooden floor in his heavy boots. 'Midnight, girls. Off to bed wit' ya,' he says.

I follow Dewey back upstairs to a bedroom. I tell her I'm sorry for upsetting her and she forgives me instantly again. There are two large beds with iron frames and Kathleen and Mary are tucked up together in one of them. So I must be sharing with Dewey. This'll be strange, but at least it's Dewey.

'I'll do your hair, Fan,' she says. 'I need your brush, Mary.' She takes a large brush of burnished metal and thick bristles from the chest of drawers.

Mary tuts. 'What about your own brush, Dew?'

I freeze, wondering how Mary and Kathleen will react when Dewey tells them I threw the ivory brush so hard that it broke. They don't have many nice things from what I've seen. At home I can hardly shut my wardrobe because it's so full of clothes and random stuff.

'I dropped it,' says Dewey. 'It broke.'

'Oh, heavens!' says Kathleen. 'But that was your birthday present.'

'These things happen. I'll live.'

I feel awful, even though I think that having something made of ivory is as bad as having a fur coat. Dewey's a nice sister not to dob on me.

Maisy pops into my head, because we're always trying to get each other into trouble. I pop her out again before I get upset in front of everyone.

The springs of the bed creak as Dewey and I sit on the edge. I'm used to having short hair so having my hair brushed is a strange sensation at first, but Dewey is gentle.

While she's plaiting it, I remember the coins in Fan's carpetbag. I wonder how much an ivory hairbrush would cost.

'Time for sleep, girls,' says Mary. She blows out the candle suddenly. I get in under the sheet and quilt next to Dewey.

'Cuddle up, Fan,' she whispers.

The moon is low and full, throwing a silver light on our bed. I feel stiff and strange, frightened to go to sleep in 1908.

Then something worse strikes me. Why didn't I think of this before now? I've got no choice but to ask Dewey, even if it threatens to blow my cover.

'Dew,' I whisper. 'I need to...' I pause, panicking about which words to use. I go with what my gran says. 'Nature's calling.'

'Eh?'

No good, I'll try what Dad says: 'The dunny.'

Dew yawns and turns over in bed. 'Just use the

chamber-pot, and shush now, Fan. I'm bone-tired.'

'It's under our bed,' whispers one of the girls from the other side of the room.

My face heats up. I can't pee into a bowl in a room that three other people are in! I get out of bed, determined to find a proper toilet.

Mary props herself up on her elbow. 'Here, take the candle if you're going to the dunny. And mind the Dunny Man doesn't catch you!' All three girls giggle. Could this get any worse? What's a Dunny Man? Maybe it's made up, like the Tooth Fairy, but for poo.

I creep through the kitchen and down the back stairs where I saw Frankie take the dead rat. In a yard there's a leaning shed with a corrugated roof and doors into two cubicles. Both have a wooden bench with a hole cut in the middle and there's a small stack of newspapers that I think is meant to be toilet paper. I go into one, put the candle in the corner and close the door, hitching up my nightie.

I can see the moon over the top of the door, high above the roof of the pub. I miss home and as my lip wobbles, hot tears roll down my face again. I can't do this. I can't!

But after I've cried for a bit, I gulp down the sadness like a pill and a laugh pops out. Because look at me! I'm on a dunny by candlelight in 1908! And at least the

Duracks are kind and funny. Maybe I *can* get through this. I have to believe there's a reason, and that there's a way back if I can find out more about what happened at Wylie's Baths.

Even if I feel like falling apart, I won't.

14

Morning

It's dark when I wake, and for a second I hope that when I stretch out my legs I'll find Dewey's feet and I'll be home. But there's no Dewey. My hair's still short. And I'm still in the future.

Last night I couldn't sleep. I was all jittery like I am before a race. It didn't help that music was playing somewhere on the street and cars were whirring past all night. I lay there and tried to work out how I came to be here. I'm sure it was something to do with Wylie's Baths. So the plan this morning is to get up before anyone else and sneak back there. I have to get home. I'll never make State if I'm stuck here. And as nice as everyone is in 2021, I miss my family.

I get up and go out to the kitchen area in the dark, letting my eyes adjust like they do at home. Then, because I can spark light with just a switch, I do and the room is flooded with bright light. No candles or gas lamps; this is electricity, which is rarely used in private houses. Mina is the only person I know who has it. Ma would love this.

I wonder what she'd make of the food in the can that we had for dinner last night. Father opened it with a metal contraption and poured the contents into a bowl and put it in a large box with a window at the front. He pressed some buttons, there was a ding and it was ready. The dinner was cooked in seconds. I keep imagining what Ma would do with all the time she'd save. She could swim at the baths with me. She could read. She could eat biscuits from a box. Or make tea from a bag.

I am missing home like an ache, but there are such wonders here, and Cat's family is kind. I know I would learn much from them if I stayed, but I have to get back to my family.

I decide to eat before I leave. I take out two slices of the fluffy white bread and stick them in the top of the metal box Father called the toaster. They sit up, not descending into the box like they did last night. I stare at them, hoping they will behave as they should. Nothing happens. I push at the buttons. The bread drops in. I watch. Seconds later the bread pops up brown and hot.

Here there is butter as rich as cream. No dripping or lard to be seen. There are jams and something called

Vegemite too. I take that down from the shelf. Sniff the top. It's brown and salty and I stick my finger in to taste.

At first, I want to spit it into the sink. It's like day-old overcooked stew, but as my mouth adjusts I find I quite like it.

I learned a few things about Cat from Maisy. Except for Lucy all of her friends are at her old school, which is far away. She's on a scholarship for swimming and she can only stay at the school if her times are good. Maisy doesn't think Cat is very committed.

I discovered that there is a mother but that she is away, working. I couldn't get to the bottom of that, but obviously things are very different in this future world.

I have been wondering, too, where the real Cat is. I know she didn't go training yesterday morning because the first thing Maisy asked me when she found me at school was where I'd been. And last night Maisy wanted to know if I 'wagged' training so I could lie in bed watching Netflix, or meet a boy. I had no answers for her. I don't know this Netflix. And I don't know if Cat knows any boys.

But I also don't know where Cat was for those hours.

After all my questions, Maisy was particularly suspicious when I offered to brush her hair. I promised not to pull the knots. She finally let me and it was nice. I only hit a few snags and managed to do a special braid down her back. She seemed happy, which made me giggle, because at home my sisters are always doing whatever they can to avoid being stuck with me fixing their hair.

I had something called a shower too. I didn't have to heat the water, I just turned a tap, and it ran so hot I had to turn the other one too until it cooled down. They don't make their own soap and they have liquid shampoo just for washing their hair. It comes in bottles and it smells so sweet like the flowers near the Lavender Bay baths. I used a handful and it foamed all over my head and I had to wash it out from my eyes because it stung a little.

'You're up early, Cat,' whispers Father, shutting the door so Maisy can sleep.

I should have snuck away without stopping to eat bread.

'Morning, Fath—Dad,' I say.

He takes down two cups from the cupboard, fills up a metal jug with water and presses a red button on the side.

'There's no training this morning. Thought you'd be in the land of the dead!'

'Dead?' I ask, alarmed.

He laughs. 'Sleeping, like your sister!'

'Oh,' I smile. 'I thought I might go to Wylie's Baths.'

'Where?'

I shrug, trying to copy Maisy who uses shrugs to explain things instead of using words.

He laughs and the sound is light, like Da's laugh sometimes. 'In Coogee?' he asks. 'It's a bit quicker to go to the local pool.'

I nod and focus on my toast. Once I leave he doesn't have to know I'm actually going to Wylie's.

'Excellent! Coach will be happy. Let me have my cuppa and I'll drive you.'

'I can get there,' I tell him.

'We're not in Orange anymore. You can't wander the streets of Surry Hills alone at five in the morning.'

I have no idea what Orange is other than a colour, but I know better than to admit it. It must be a place we lived—they lived. Strange that Surry Hills is dangerous now, when it seems so clean and modern. No cases of the plague or infestation of rats here.

Obviously making my way to Wylie's Baths will have to wait because Father isn't going to let me go alone. I'll have to try later in the day.

'I'll go and wake Maisy,' I say. But first I make my new sister a cup of sweet tea. Carrying it in to her, I switch on the lights, like Father did, causing Maisy to growl and burrow under her pillow.

'I made you tea. We're going swimming!'

She lifts her blankets and peeps at me. 'You did?'

'Three sugars! Is that…cool?' I try out the new word and like how it rolls off my tongue.

'Three? Wow. Thanks, Cat,' she says taking the cup from me. I perch on the end of her bed.

'Why are we swimming today? You do everything you can to miss training, and now when you could be sleeping, you want to swim. I don't understand you, Cat,' she says.

'That makes two of us,' I tell her lightly.

She slurps her tea and watches me suspiciously.

The car ride is gripping. I should be scared but I'm not. I press the little button on the window so it goes down and up and down again and I hang my head out and feel the cool morning air in my face, until Maisy tells me a little gruesomely that we'll pass a truck and I'll be beheaded.

The car is much finer than a tram. The seats are soft and comfortable and there's even music playing inside. We sort of glide along like the car's on skates. I can't stop smiling.

'You're happy this morning, Cat,' says Father looking at me in the mirror.

'Am I?' This Cat person must be cranky, not as happy as I am to be riding in the back of a car.

We pull up outside a large building. It's impressive and nothing like any of the pools I've ever seen. I fling the car door open and try to get out, forgetting I have a strap across my waist and get all tangled and stuck. Father leans back and snaps the button so I come free and fall out of the door, laughing. My new family look at me oddly and I vow to try to be more like Cat. If only I knew what she was like.

Father holds the door to the large building open and I follow Maisy inside. There's a strange smell and the air is thick and swampy. Father stops and chats to the man at the counter. I walk after Maisy trying to look like I know where I'm going.

Then I see the pool. It's enormous and the water looks so clear and blue. There are long ropes separating the lanes and people swimming up and down and I can't get over how clean it looks.

'Coming, Cat?'

I hurry after my new sister. She takes off her clothes at the side of the pool and dumps them. I immediately start folding them, imagining what Ma would say.

'What are you doing?'

'Oh, sorry, just trying to neaten up.'

Maisy tilts her head like she's trying to work me out. I toss Maisy's clothes in the air and they scatter on the seat. She laughs at me. 'That's more like it!' she says.

I watch as she stretches a strange green thing onto her head, tucking her long ponytail up inside it. What is this cap made of and why is it so tight and bright? I wonder.

'Are you swimming or what?' Maisy asks.

I quickly take off my outer layers, feeling very underdressed in this skimpy piece of fabric, but at least this time my stomach isn't bare. I don't know if I need a cap too but I'm not sure where mine is, so I skip after Maisy who is already in the water and fitting some glasses across her face.

'You look funny!' I tell her playfully.

She dives under the water and starts swimming breaststroke down the pool. She's strong, her body arches well and her legs hardly break the surface.

I dive in and chase after her, wanting to see what my new body can do. My arms don't reach the same distance and my head comes up too quickly for breath. I try to find a rhythm but it is hard swimming with someone else's limbs.

My hand hits the wall and I look up to see Maisy has already turned. She's faster than I expected. Come on, Cat, I tell myself. You can go quicker than this. I set off again.

As soon as I hit my stride, there's a whispering sound. The words are hard to make out and I can't tell where they're coming from, but I can hear them under the water. I stop mid-stroke to look around. The whispering stops. I have the lane to myself. I must have imagined it. I plunge under the water again.

The hand unwinds...

That time I heard it properly! Are the words inside my head? I don't know what they mean. I keep going, swimming as fast as I can. *The hand unwinds...the hand unwinds.* It seems I can't outswim the whispering *or* catch up with Maisy. She turns in a neat flip underwater when she reaches the end and keeps going. I power after her. Three more laps up and down, until I find her waiting for me.

'You're slow today,' she says as I glide in. 'And where are your goggles?'

'Goggles?'

'Yes. These things remember!' She slides hers up so I can see her eyes.

'Oh! Goggles.' I smile. 'Not sure. Could you hear something just then? A voice saying something about hands and winding—no, *un*winding?'

'What on earth are you talking about?'

'Forget it,' I say. She hasn't a clue. I hoped the whispering message might be some new magic of modern swimming pools, but it can't be if I'm the only one who can hear it.

'Cat, you've been acting strangely...'

'Since yesterday? I know.'

Maisy shakes her head. 'No, I mean extra strange

since yesterday, but you've seemed weird about swimming for weeks. It's like you don't care if you're slow anymore. You were fast in the heats, but then you wagged training. I don't get it.'

'I'm not trying to swim slow!' I say. I wish I knew why Cat wagged training. I'm convinced it has something to do with wherever she is now.

'Fine. Come on then. I'll race you again,' she tells me.

She pulls her goggles over her eyes and takes off. I know how to beat her. Even Mina can't always keep up if I swim trudgen.

I swim as hard as I can, like I'm back at Lavender Bay and, instead of Maisy, it's Dorothy and Mina beside me. My arms power through the water and my feet scissor kick like I'm at the Olympics. I can't see Maisy but I bet she's miles back. This time there's no voice in my head.

I touch the end and leap up, grinning.

'What. Was. *That?!*'

I realise that Maisy touched the end before me.

'You beat me,' I say.

'Yeah. Dad could beat you swimming like that! Don't let Coach see you swim like that! You'll be off the team!'

'But...' I try, but Maisy is already powering back down the pool. Obviously I've done something else wrong, but I have absolutely no idea what it is.

15

Wash Day

Someone's shaking me. I peel open one eye expecting to see Maisy dressed for training.

'You were talking in your sleep, Fan,' says Dewey.

So I'm still here, and still *her*.

'What did I say?' I ask, all groggy in my throat.

'You kept saying *the hand unwinds* over and over. What were you dreaming?'

'I don't remember.'

'Well, c'mon, lazybones. It's wash day.'

'Sleepy,' I mumble. I pull a pillow over my head. It's heavy and smells like a farm.

'Stop acting the maggot, Fan. Get ready before Ma skins us. Kath and Mary have already started.'

Outside there are unfamiliar sounds mixed in with calling voices, the clatter of trams, horses' hooves and bicycle bells. I peek out from under the pillow to see Dewey pulling the sheets off the other bed like she's done it a thousand times. She feels like a friend, and I have a sudden urge to spill.

'Dewey...I have to tell you something.'

'Mm?' She piles sheets into a large basket.

'But you might not believe me.'

'Is it about your race on Saturday, Fan? Because you've told me fifteen times that you're going to win it and *I believe you*, all right?' She laughs and hoists the basket onto her hip. The words 'race on Saturday' strike a new fear into me.

'What race?'

She rolls her eyes. 'Come on, strip the bed. I know you're up for the State team, but the sheets won't wash themselves.'

I can't believe it. Fanny's going for State just like I was before this thing happened. What does that mean? Are we connected somehow? Is she sleeping in my bed like I'm sleeping in hers, or am I in both places at once? I wish I knew what was happening. I feel completely alone.

I'm back to thinking that telling Dewey would be a mistake. Maybe she's more likely to help me if she thinks I'm her sister. If I tried to tell her what was going on, she could tell Ma and Da and they'd lock me up. Old books are full of girls and women being locked up in asylums for being mad, that's what Mum always says.

I must find out more about yesterday. I wish I could Google, but all I have is Dewey. Was anyone else at the baths? Have other strange things happened there? What if I swam into a kind of Bermuda Triangle? I need to do some detective work.

'Dewey, did you think I was fast yesterday, at training?'

'Very. But I wish you were faster with those sheets.' She starts to peel them off while I'm still sitting on the bed.

'Who else was there?'

'Only Mr Wylie, right at the end when he came for the watch.'

'The watch—you mean, he came to watch me?'

'The stopwatch, Fan,' she says, yanking the sheet from under me. 'Would you help?'

The stopwatch. For the first time, I think about the one Maisy found in Aunt Rachel's things. I had it with me yesterday morning. Is it a clue?

'What did it look like?' I ask, realising as soon as it's out how strange I must sound and then fumbling more questions to cover myself. 'I mean, *er*, what did you like about it? Was it the pretty silver case?'

'Sure, nice enough. But the button was stiff and I had to use both thumbs. Come on, I'm taking the basket to Mary.'

Mr Wylie's stopwatch. The words I was saying in my sleep. I'm covered in goosebumps! I must go back to Wylie's Baths.

I grab Dewey by each arm. 'Cover for me. I have to go out.'

'Have you lost your mind, Fan? We'll be lucky if we finish the washing by dark as it is.'

'You don't understand. I need to train, Dewey. For the race. State trials! Please, you know how important this is to me,' I say with desperation. I have got to follow the clues and get to Wylie's.

Dewey pulls away. She looks angry for the first time since I met her.

'You can't leave, Fan. It's not fair.'

'But this is more important than anything!'

'If I can miss school on wash day, you can miss swimming. If Ma, Kath and Mary can do it week after week their whole lives, so can you. I know you love swimming more than anything else in the world, but this is life.'

Dewey leaves, tearful and fuming. I'm more alone than ever without her. And I can't believe that washing sheets comes before everything else that a girl might want to do.

'There you are!' says Kath when I finally skulk into the

kitchen. It wasn't easy getting dressed. It took ages—everything's ribbons and buttons.

Kath's kneading dough on the table. 'I'll finish this and then I'll be down to help.' She jerks her head but I've no idea what I'm supposed to do now.

'Fan! Stop daydreaming and get to the scullery!'

I follow her eyes to the doorway off the kitchen. Through there is the staircase down to the yard where the dunny is. A sound of laughter comes from the yard, and eventually I find a small room at the back of the pub.

'At last,' says Mary. 'Check the copper, Fan. Should be hot by now.'

I work out that the 'copper' is the large bricked area with a huge pot inside and a lid on the top, an iron door in the side and glimpses of a fire burning in a cavernous hole at the bottom. There's a pile of logs next to it. I lift the wooden lid and get a face full of steam.

'Hurry, Fan!' says Mary, looking cross with a huge sheet hanging off a long broom handle.

I don't know what I'm meant to do.

'What's the matter with her today?' says Mary.

'She'd rather be swimming,' Dewey says in a flat tone without looking at me.

Mary tuts. 'Well I'd rather be Cleopatra. It's already five-thirty, Fan, can you wake up and get moving?'

'Would you believe me when I say I've forgotten what I'm supposed to do?'

She rolls her eyes. 'As a matter of fact I would. Fetch the bucket and fill that tub with hot water before I shove this somewhere the sun doesn't shine.'

It's going to be a long day.

Wash day was close to the worst experience of my life. It took four of us eight hours. Eight hours! It wasn't just our beds—it was all the guest beds that had to be stripped and washed too. We stopped for breakfast and lunch, except Ma called lunch *dinner*. I sweated so much I didn't need to use the dunny once. Weird perk of being dehydrated! Mary said it was lucky we had a scorcher of a day so the sheets could dry—and I thought, what about us, walking around this yard like burning-hot zombies?

Now we're on folding: lovely, relaxing folding—much nicer than boiling, soaking, stoking the fire, rubbing sheets on the washboard with hard soap and getting your knuckles scraped, rinsing, mangling, hanging the heavy tubs on the yard walls, scrubbing the scullery floor.

Tomorrow is ironing day, which is another very good reason I need to get out of here. This work feels like a way to stop girls from doing anything else! Back home

I can always predict when Dad's about to ask me to load the dishwasher and I usually choose that moment to start a long hot shower to get out of it.

'You're so quiet today, Fan,' says Mary, as we fold a sheet together.

Kath jumps in. 'She's thinking about Saturday's race. It's the only thing that shuts her up.'

'True!' Mary presses the folded sheet into my chest and brushes my cheek with the back of her hand. The sisters are all so sweet to each other. And Dewey didn't stay grumpy with me for long.

Am I *ever* sweet to Maisy? I feel squirmy when I imagine the Durack sisters overhearing one of our arguments.

'Dewey and Fan, Borax time!' Ma yells from the kitchen.

'Lucky you,' Kath says.

This could be good. As I follow Dew up the stairs I wonder if Borax is some kind of hot drink. My gran drinks something called Bovril, which I never fancied, but if it means I finally get to sit down I'll try anything.

Turns out Borax is a kind of poison!

Dewey and I are sent to the bedrooms to paint every inch of the iron bed-frames with this strange-smelling substance. It's hard to keep asking questions without sounding mad, but I get inventive.

'Can you believe we have to do...*Borax*?' I say, on my hands and knees with a paintbrush.

'I know, but Ma reckons the only thing that's keeping us from another plague are good habits like this.'

'The plague...right.' I shudder, thinking of the pandemic in my own time, and paint a lot more thoroughly than I was before.

I'm outside alone now, in the constant ding-a-ling of trams, horse-drawn carts, and cars that bounce and splutter. I even crossed the road—there are no traffic lights so it was like being inside a computer game with only one life. At first I wanted to head to Wylie's Baths, but after I thought about it I realised I need to plan more carefully. So while I'm working on that I'm going to find somewhere that sells hairbrushes, race back to the pub and give Dewey a present. I owe her.

Can I call it a present if I'm replacing something I broke? Maybe I'll get her something extra as well. And a treat for Kath and Mary. And something for rat-boy Frankie. Though I suppose it's not fair to leave out the others. Da and Ma, stern John and cheeky Con, and Mick, who reminds me of some of the boys back in Orange I used to muck around with. I hope these brown coins buy enough to go round.

16

Buttons

It's lunchtime and Lucy is watching me work my way through three bowls of food. She has picked around the outside of her meal, but I'm scoffing mine down so nobody takes it.

'Doesn't that spag bol have meat in it?' says Lucy.

'Tastes a bit like rabbit.'

'Since when do you eat meat?' She leans closer to my bowl and inspects the sauce. 'I doubt it's rabbit. We could run tests in the lab. Imagine the outrage if it was!'

Lucy is as confounding as my new sister, but at least she's enthusiastic and friendly.

'I like rabbit,' I tell her, with a mouthful of slippery long worms. I slurp it up and sauce flicks onto Lucy's nose.

'You're strange, Cat. Even more than usual.' She wipes her nose with her sleeve, and then wipes the sleeve with her other sleeve.

'Sorry,' I say.

'I don't mind. As long as you are ready for our science presentation.'

Closing my eyes, I try to imagine what a presentation would be. In swimming winners are presented with hairclips and the like, but I doubt that's what Lucy is talking about.

'Cat? Are you?'

I open my eyes as wide as I can to show her that I'm keen.

'Cat! This is important.' She plunges her head into her hands.

Worried, I poke her.

She looks up at me. 'I'm thinking. You can be my assistant. Then all you have to do is hand me the important elements and work the overhead projector and demonstrate. Okay?' She waves her arms around looking serious.

I wonder how to ask her what an overhead projector is. I make a guess that it's a contraption that sits above my head. 'Can you show me where the overhead projector is?'

'Cat! What is wrong with you? We've been through all this.'

'I have to apologise. I'm not feeling myself,' I tell Lucy, wishing I could just tell her everything. But I fear what will happen if I did. How can I prove that the person who looks like Cat and sounds like Cat is not Cat?

Someone bumps into my back as they walk past with their tray and I hear giggling. It's a girl with long brown hair and she looks at me strangely.

'Oops, sorry Catherine,' she says, like my name is not something she wants to say.

'That's okay,' I say.

As she walks off with her friends, Lucy whispers to me, 'You hate her! What are you doing?'

'Why?' I can't imagine hating anyone, or at least not admitting it to someone else. Ma always encourages us to keep our bad feelings about people to ourselves.

'Honestly, Cat. I'm not even sure who you are today! I'll see you in class. I'm going to set up.'

Lucy sounds as frustrated with me as Ma does when I miss my chores, so I finish eating the worms, which I've now learned are actually made of flour and water, which is a big relief. Then I head off after Lucy, pleased that I at least know where the Science classroom is because I saw it yesterday.

'Hey, Cat,' I hear behind me and I turn to see the girl I'm supposed to hate skipping towards me.

'You training tomorrow?' she asks me.

I should have guessed she was a swimmer. 'Of

course,' I say.

'Still want to swim the fourth leg in the relay?'

My new plan for any questions that I don't know how to answer is to reply with a question of my own. 'Why?' I ask.

She frowns. 'Because your times have slipped, or had you forgotten?'

This girl must be like Cat's version of Mina. Although Mina and I are playful in our rivalry, we are still always trying to beat each other. Cat swims the final leg because she's the fastest—the fastest always takes the last leg. This girl wants to steal that honour. Not a chance!

'I trained this morning. I'm making a comeback,' I tell her with a smile.

'We'll see.' She returns the smile but it doesn't quite reach her eyes and it makes me wonder what's going on. 'By the way I'm having a party,' she says and thrusts a piece of paper into my hands, before rushing off down the hall to catch someone else.

I keep walking towards the classrooms and read the paper as I go. If everyone else walks along not looking where they're going, then I might as well too.

The party is on Saturday. I'm a little confused by the meaning of some words like *this party is going to be lit*. Does it mean there will be a fire? The only party

I've ever been to was the one that Mina's father held to celebrate the opening of the baths. This party seems to be for a birthday, which I've only ever celebrated with a lie-in and no chores.

'All good, Cat?' Lucy asks as I walk into the classroom.

I hold out the piece of paper.

She reads the words and shakes her head. 'Rebecca? No. You're. Not!'

'There might be cake,' I say lightly, hoping to soften my friend.

She rolls her eyes and turns around to show me some contraption. 'This is the projector. Button here. Button here. Press this one to move through the slides. Press this one to pause. Got it? For the lights, you need to press this one.' She's joking, as if she knows she doesn't need to tell me.

I laugh as if I knew all along. But at least I know now that that is the overhead projector.

'Good. This is worth half our marks. It needs to be exceptional! Strike that, it needs to be perfect.'

Lucy is clearly as committed to learning as I am to swimming. She keeps talking about our presentation as the rest of the students file in, chatting and whispering.

The teacher tells us we can make a start and Lucy welcomes the class and then begins talking about something called climate change and explaining that the global water temperatures are increasing. I'd like to understand more about this, but I know I can't interrupt. Lucy looks very serious and her voice is calm and steady.

She pauses her speech and nods at me. I think I'm supposed to press a button. So I do.

'Wrong one!' hisses Lucy.

I quickly press the other button and the wall behind Lucy flares with bright white light. She glares at me—I've obviously pressed another wrong button, so I try the blue one.

Someone starts laughing as the wall goes black and then white again.

'Fix it, Cat! It's the other button,' barks Lucy.

I leap forward to press the only button I haven't tried and instead I slam into the projector and it bumps off the stand and crashes onto the floor.

And Lucy says words I've only ever heard men say. And not the sort of men Ma would let me talk to. This time there's a lot of laughter.

Lucy hasn't spoken to me all afternoon. It's almost as bad as the day I broke Ma's favourite vase, the one she brought over on the boat from Ireland. But at least I knew that Ma would speak to me eventually. Lucy might never talk to me again.

I'm not sure how I'll make it up to her. If only I could get back to 1908, then I'd never have to see anyone from Victoria Grammar again, which I know is cowardly, but it's hard pretending to be someone else all the time. I just want to be me.

The bell has gone and instead of waiting for Maisy, I'm hurrying away from school as fast as I can. I'm going to Wylie's Baths. I want to see something familiar. And it's the place where I became Cat, so maybe there will be a clue there about how I can get back to being me.

I reach the busy street corner. A man with hair longer than Dewey's is sitting cross-legged on the ground and playing a guitar. He has a hat in front of him with coins in it, and a sleeping dog beside him. He grins at me and I see he's missing a tooth. He reminds me of the men who drink in our pub. I nod and hurry past.

I wonder what Dewey is doing right now. If she's missing me or if she hasn't even realised I'm gone. Maybe Cat is in my time pretending to be me while I'm here pretending to be her. I hope she's doing a better job of it.

The first glimpse of the water is soothing and I rush towards the green grass hill that heads down to the sea. Automatically I look to my right for Mina's house, but it's not where it should be. Instead some large grey building has eaten her lovely house, and it makes me sad. Does nothing from my time remain?

I hurry past the children kicking a ball around and rush to the entrance of the baths. I have no money to get in so I will have to run fast through the turnstile. But when I reach the little entrance that is both familiar and not, there is a rope hanging across blocking entry with a yellow sign that tells of the baths being closed, and of the work being done on the far ocean wall. Ahead I can see a bronze statue of a girl, but from here all I can see is her back.

I slide under the rope that barricades the entrance and hurry down the stairs to the baths.

The sea air smells strong and for a second I'm lost in my surroundings. Then a man in large orange overalls waves me away.

'Baths closed,' he shouts up at me.

If the way back is through Wylie's, then it looks like I'm spending another night in 2021.

Getting home to the shop takes ages but I'm so saddened that I don't even pause for sweets when I get inside. I trudge upstairs, wanting to cry but also knowing that if I start, I might never stop.

'I covered for you,' says Maisy hearing me come in. 'Told Dad you had to go to Lucy's for a project.'

She smiles at me from the end of her bed.

'Thanks.'

'Where have you been?'

'Trying to get home,' I tell her, wanting to be honest for just one second.

'Oh. You hate it here don't you?'

I shake my head. 'No. I just don't belong.'

'I always felt like that in Orange,' she tells me, bending her knees up to make room for me. Talking to Maisy makes me miss Dewey even more.

'Why?' I ask.

She shrugs. 'Back in Orange I always felt like I was just your little sister. It's different here,' she says.

'You shouldn't care what people think.'

She gives me a look that tells me this is not what Cat would say, so I aim for changing the conversation. 'I'm going to get started on dinner. Want to help me?'

She laughs. 'Cook? You? What are we having? Two-minute noodles?'

'I was going to make a rabbit pie,' I say, really wanting to know what two-minute noodles are.

'Gross, no. I am *not* eating rabbit.'

I laugh at the expression on her face. 'Okay. No rabbit. What sort of meat would you eat?'

'Chicken.'

Do I have to pluck it? Snap its neck? Or will there be

a can of chicken in the cupboard, I wonder.

'But what are *you* having for dinner?' Maisy asks as if I would never eat chicken.

'Chicken pie!'

Maisy looks surprised. 'What happened to "saving the world" one chicken at a time?'

I decide now is a good time to shrug. Maisy shakes her head like I'm the most frustrating person alive.

The fridge is stacked full of boxes and bottles and jars but nothing that says chicken. I try the magic ice cupboard at the top and here I find all sorts of things but still no chicken. Then I remember I live above a shop.

Dashing down the stairs, I wait for Father to finish serving a customer. 'Where would I find chicken?'

'Why?'

'I'm cooking dinner!'

'Does it have to be chicken?'

'It has to be meat for a pie. Maisy suggested chicken,' I tell him.

He slides his glasses up onto the top of his head and rubs the bridge of his nose. 'You don't eat meat, Cat, and you don't cook. Am I missing something?'

Now I understand Maisy's comment. 'People change,' I say.

He nods at me like he's trying to be serious.

'Apparently so. There should be chuck beef in the fridge. You can use that for a pie.'

'Would I cook it like rabbit?'

This time he laughs and the sound is lovely. I can't help but join in. Obviously rabbit is not something people eat in the future. They don't know what they're missing.

'Probably. Yes.'

'Okay,' I say, starting to go back up the stairs. Then I remember that I'm hungry.

'Any potato scallops lying around?'

Dad reaches into the hot glass box and throws one my way. 'Think quick!' he says.

I catch it and smile at him. As much as I miss my family, being Cat isn't all bad.

It takes all the cupboards banging and the fridge door opening four times for me to find the ingredients I need. Everything is in packets and wrappings and nothing is recognisable. While I wait for the pastry to settle, I sweep and scrub and tidy all the rooms, except for Father's.

I'm making the filling for the pie when Maisy comes out of our room and leans against the kitchen table. She looks around. 'Since when do you clean?'

How much more could I get wrong? 'Since today! I'm trying to be better around the house,' I tell her, deciding to put my love of acting to good use. 'I couldn't find chicken. It's going to be a beef pie. Is that okay?'

Maisy shrugs. 'Sure.'

'Do you have a cookbook anywhere?'

'No, *we* don't. Just Google it.'

'Google it?'

She wiggles her fingers in the air like she's making them dance. I smile.

'Look it up on Google. You know, on your laptop,' she says slowly.

She must mean the silver thing that Lucy was using in English class. So I have one of those too. I wonder where it is. I want to ask her how a *laptop* knows things. Is it like a giant library in one small box? But I can't risk any more of Maisy's confused looks.

'Where is your laptop, Cat? I haven't seen it for a few days.'

'Um…gone.'

Her eyes grow wide and worried, like that's even worse than being slow in the pool. 'What do you mean *gone*?'

'I left it at Lucy's,' I tell her, hoping that if Ma ever learns of all my fibs she will forgive me.

'What about your phone? It's always beeping and I haven't heard it.'

'That's at Lucy's too,' I say. 'I left everything at

Lucy's! Even my brain.' I try for a laugh, but Maisy is watching me suspiciously. Now I'm wondering where Cat has left these precious things.

'Did you leave Aunt Rachel's stopwatch there too? I haven't seen it since the other night. I want to see if I can fix it,' Maisy says.

'Why, what happened to it?' I ask.

'You saw what happened! You don't have to make me feel even worse!'

'I'm not trying to, honest.'

'Well, we both know I broke it, and that it's probably a really old antique and Aunt Rachel will be upset. The timer hand started going anticlockwise after the button jammed.'

Anticlockwise? *The hand unwinds.* Whose voice did I hear in the pool? Was it Cat trying to tell me something? I have to find her missing things, especially the stopwatch.

I wipe the bench, trying to calm my racing heart and wring the cloth out in the sink.

Maisy is looking at me with narrowed eyes. 'Are you okay, Cat?'

'Yes,' I tell her. Another lie. I fold the cloth and put it on the side of the sink, thinking about something I could say to stop Maisy focusing on me. 'You're fast in the pool, Maisy. Very fast.'

'Really?'

'Maybe better than me.'

'Really?'

'Really.'

She frowns like she doesn't trust me, but I reply, 'I won't lie about swimming. Swimming is the most important thing of all. And you're good. I promise.'

'Thanks, Cat. That means—' She stops, seeming to be struggling with the words.

Nodding, I say, 'I know.'

'Do you want to borrow my phone? You know, to Google it?'

Do I? 'Okay.'

'Here,' she says, handing it to me. 'Password's lane 2.'

I take her phone in my hand and stare at it. This feels a little like pressing the wrong buttons on the overhead projector. I tentatively push the one near the bottom and things light up, but I have no idea how to get magic answers from it. I see numbers blinking and realise that's the time. How does this thing know what time it is? What other secrets does it know? I slide it back on the bench. I'm not ready for this yet. My pie will have to be Google-free.

17

Note

I'm shopping in 1908 and dying to text Luce and Tam about it.

I've come to a chemist that looks like a potions lab: rows of bottles and jars up to the ceiling, smart glass cabinets, hundreds of little drawers and an intense whiff of wood-panelling. On the counter there's a pestle and mortar like the one we have on our kitchen bench at home. Ours usually has keys and hairbands in it, though.

There's one other customer: a woman with the largest pram I've ever seen. Behind the counter stands a man in a stiff suit, wearing small round glasses right at the end of his nose. The woman scoops her crying baby out of the pram and puts it into some large scales. While they have a boring chat about the baby, I take a look around. I can see a few combs but there's nothing like the brush I broke. I don't know what I can get any of the others in here but there's a lolly shop next door.

It's my turn—the woman leaves with a bright blue bottle, jiggling her cranky baby in the giant pram. I hope the potion works; that is a terrible noise.

'Yes, Miss?' says the man.

'Hello, I need a hairbrush. Something pretty. It's for my sister.'

'We have a number of hairbrushes, Miss.'

He's very serious. In a swift move he pulls out a tray. There are several hairbrushes and one of them looks exactly like the one I broke. I run my finger over it, thinking about the poor dead elephant whose tusks were stolen.

'We have the full vanity set in that design, if Miss would care to see it.'

'But it's cruelty to animals,' I say.

The man lets out a brittle laugh and when I look up he's giving me a patronising glare.

'Miss, it is resin. It merely looks like bone. Resin is far more affordable.' He clears his throat. 'Could Miss really afford ivory?' He sniggers again. Can he tell that I'm not rich, then? Maybe it's my accent, or my scruffy hat and boots. I think he's rude and before I can stop myself I say, 'I'll take it. And the matching mirror. And I'd like some hand cream. Something that smells nice.' Help, what am I doing? I have no idea how much this will cost.

The man wraps the mirror and brush in tissue paper, and then a bottle labelled Pond's Angel Skin. He's doing everything in slow motion. Sweat trickles down my spine as I worry that I won't be able to pay for it. When he says the price I tip the contents of my purse onto the counter. He huffs and picks up four coins, leaving two. Phew!

I pick up the packages, still annoyed with the man.

'Good-*day*, Sir,' I say, forcefully.

Once I'm outside I get the giggles. I want to tell someone what just happened—my spectacularly cutting 'Good-day, Sir'. I think I got that from a movie.

In the lolly shop, I hold out the coins and say, 'Hello, what can I get with this?'

'A bit of this, a bit of that,' says a woman in a white apron. She's very wrinkled with a wide smile and not many teeth.

'Yes please.' I put the last two coins in her hand. She fills a brown paper bag with liquorice straps and striped lollies, and when I ask for a few extra bags so I can make separate presents for my family, she calls me a lovely young lass. Lovely! Me!

I still feel lovely when I get back to the pub. Most of the family are in the kitchen, except for Da, Con and John. I give Ma her hand cream first.

She whacks me on the arm. 'What did you get me

this for?' But straight afterwards she wraps her arms around me and squeezes tight. Then she whacks me again! And finally she opens the bottle for a sniff. I think she's happy.

Mick and Frankie say they're off to trade with their lollies. Mary and Kath suck on liquorice straps as I give the biggest package to Dewey. Her face lights up.

'I can't believe you got me these, Fan. They're beautiful!'

'You're welcome.'

'But how did you afford it?'

'Oh, I had some money.'

'But wasn't that for your race entry tomorrow?' says Kath. 'From Da doing the whip-round in the pub. Where did you get more from?'

My smile sticks. I'm in trouble. It's only just hit me that the coins weren't really mine, even though I was trying to be kind. They're all looking at me and I've got to come up with a reason for why I apparently had 'extra' money.

Brainwave—thank you, brain.

'From Arthur.'

'Arthur Gon?' says Mary. 'Con's friend?' Mary's cheeks are pink. Maybe she's got a crush on him.

'The Chinese lad?' says Ma, with an edge in her voice.

'He's nice,' Mary says defensively. 'Very proper manners. He's studying to be a doctor.'

'A Chinese doctor in this fair country, that'll be a first.' Ma frowns.

They all start to discuss Arthur, his family and the Chinese people who live in Sydney, and it's awful how judgmental and racist they sound. They feel like strangers again. I can't just stand here, and I don't care if I'm going to make them suspicious.

'You can't say things like that!' I say. Everyone stops talking and looks at me.

'Who can't?' says Ma. 'Don't tell me how to talk in my own kitchen, Sarah Francis Durack.'

'Sorry, Ma, but I believe in equality.' My voice wobbles; I want to be better at this. Then I remember something from a history lesson. 'We're Irish Catholics. There are people out there who think we're lower than them but we know it's not true. Same with Arthur. He can be anything he wants to be.'

It's very, very quiet in the kitchen.

Dewey breaks it. 'Typical Fan, biggest heart of us all.'

Kath and Mary look thoughtful.

Ma purses her lips. 'I take everyone as I find them. Didn't mean to upset you, Fanny. Now, what would Arthur Gon be giving you money for?'

'Swimming lessons. He paid up front.'

'That's grand, Fan,' says Kath. 'Just remember not to wear the club badge when you're swimming with Arthur—you know how the ladies feel about mixed bathing.'

'Too right,' Mary chips in. 'You'll never get to the Olympics if the committee finds out.'

I'm not sure if Mary's being serious—is that really Fan's ambition?

'Girls in the Olympics, indeed,' says Ma.

'But they are, Ma,' says Dewey. 'Miss Reid told us about it at school. Sailing, tennis, golf, croquet, um...'

'Archery,' adds Kath.

'That's all very well, but you don't get half-naked for any of those sports now, do you?' says Ma, and the other girls seem to agree. They go back to sniffing Ma's Angel Skin cream and eating lollies, while Dewey holds her hair close to her cheek and brushes it like it's a treasured pet.

Soon I get swept into helping to cook dinner. I know one thing that feels cooked and that's my brain. This life is too hard for me. The day is rapidly slipping away. Teatime is loud and lively. When it's time to do the dishes I'm quick and efficient but every time I finish one chore there's Ma with orders to start another.

'Con, help Fanny take the rugs to the yard for

beating!' she barks.

We have to drag six of them down the stairs and hang them in twos along the washing line in the courtyard. I haven't spent much time with Con, which is just as well because he's really good looking and in this life he's my brother: gross.

Con hands me a thing shaped like a squash racket. He walks around the other side of a rug and starts to thump it. I do the same and masses of dust flies into my face. I cough and splutter and accidentally blurt out, 'Ugh, this life is *so* not me.'

Con's beating stops over the other side of the rug.

'Is everything all right, Fan?'

'Erm, everything is'—*quick, think of something old-fashioned*—'jolly good.'

He appears suddenly, frowning. 'You seem different, lately.'

Half of me panics but the other half is happy that someone's noticed. For a moment I'm tempted to tell him.

'I'm fine. Just worried about the race. You know how I get.'

'I do. Hey, I saw Arthur today. He was asking after you. I think he likes you.'

My cheeks burn. Arthur's nice but he's much older than me. And then there's my fib about where I got the

159

extra money from. What if everyone finds out?

'I haven't got time for boys.'

'I know, swimming's all you care about. I admire you, sister, I really do.' He smiles and goes back to his side of the rug.

By the time we've finished all the chores it's pitch black outside and I'm crushed: I had this idea that I could catch a tram to Coogee before the day was over. I found out from Dewey that Mr Wylie's house is practically next to the baths and I was going to knock on the door and ask if I could borrow the stopwatch from him. It might even be the exact same one that Aunt Rachel had, and maybe the thing that made this happen. But it's too late for that plan tonight. I'll leave at dawn tomorrow because I definitely can't be Fan for her races.

So I'm stuck here for another night with a new problem to solve: how to replace the money I used to buy all the gifts? If I make it back home and the real Fan returns, she won't be able to enter the swimming carnival with no money left in her purse. I can't do that to her. The way Mary was talking earlier about the Olympics, it's obvious that Fan is as committed as you can be.

Later, when the house is dead quiet and my sisters are lightly snoring, I have an idea. But it's complicated.

I take a candle and sneak down to the bar. The till will be empty but earlier I saw where Da keeps the takings.

Now that I'm here, looking at the money, it feels wrong. I pick up a couple of coins and weigh them in my hand. The Duracks work so hard and this money isn't mine to take. But on the other hand, Da would want Fan to have it. And Fan wants to go all the way.

I can't think how else to get the money for the race.

Upstairs, I pop the coins inside the purse and leave it on the dresser. Then by candlelight I write a note to Fan and stuff that in too. I want to leave one tiny trace of myself.

Hi, this is Cat. I was you! Were you me? Good luck in the race. I hope you win. And good luck with all your dreams, never give up. I love your family, especially Dewey. I didn't love the chores, though. You can keep those! This was a weird and wonderful adventure. Cat x

I should say more but I'm stuck for what to write. A lot of my thoughts haven't made it into words yet. But somehow I feel closer to Fanny after writing to her. I wish I had a sign that she's in my life the way I'm in hers.

I can't let myself fall asleep because I want to leave before everyone else gets up. I'll lie next to Dewey and think about home. Then, when it's time, I'll creep out and go straight to Coogee.

PART 4

FREESTYLE

18
Mum

The little blue lights on the clock say 2:00. That means I have to get up in three hours to swim. I keep thinking about what it means to be stuck here, away from everyone I love. I know I need to find Cat's missing things, but I can't do that in the wee hours of the morning. I wish I could sleep.

While the pie was cooking, Dad spoke to me in his sternest voice about being more responsible and catching the bus home with Maisy instead of going to Lucy's without asking, and then he stopped because dinner smelled so delicious he couldn't concentrate.

It was not my finest pie because I was missing ingredients like suet and I had no recipe, but there were onions and carrots and some flour and seasoning and apparently it was the best thing Dad had ever eaten. I smiled at the sight of him shovelling it in like Con and Da, and that was almost enough for a few minutes. But then I thought about Dewey and my body ached to see her.

How must the real Cat be feeling if she is in my place? How must she be coping with skinning rabbits and washing clothes for hours at a time? I think I have it easier here. There are machines to wash dishes, machines to wash clothes, ovens that cook without anyone needing to stoke a fire. The meat comes in a parcel from the shop and there is no skinning required. And when I couldn't sleep, Dad poured some milk into a cup and then put it inside a box with a door and when the box dinged the milk was warm. Such wonderful magic to heat something in seconds.

I must have drifted off because the next thing I know, Maisy is shaking my shoulder.

I roll over and feel my feet hit the ground. In my dreams I'm still in Surry Hills with the sounds of the horse and cart trundling down the cobbled streets.

'I'm up, Maise,' I tell her.

'Maise?'

Tired I look up and see the frown on her face.

'Since when do you call me Maise?'

I start making my bed because I'm not sure what to say. Obviously her real sister never shortens her name.

'Since when do you make your bed? Or get up without complaining? Or cook dinner? Actually, who are you?' she says.

Forcing a laugh, I turn around and grab my new sister by the shoulders. I give her a little friendly shake. 'I'm me, silly. I'm just trying to be better.'

Maisy looks at me closely and finally nods, and I release her.

'I like this version of you!' she says.

Is this traitorous to the real Cat? Maybe I should tell Maisy the truth. Burst out with the reason I'm different. But she wouldn't believe me anyway, because it sounds so ridiculous.

Just at that second our bedroom door creaks opens and a woman steps in. She's wearing a little jacket and knee-length skirt like it's a uniform and she's smiling.

'Mum!' squeals Maisy as she throws herself at the woman.

'Hello, girls. I've missed you,' she says wrapping Maisy in a hug and holding her arms out for me to join in. I try to match my sister's excitement but it doesn't sound real when I say it. I lean in for a little hug, and then pull back letting Maisy have the moment. Hugging a mother who isn't mine when I rarely hug my own doesn't feel right.

'Are you back for ages?' Maisy asks, clinging on tight around the mother's middle. Her hair is pulled back into a bun and she has a funny little hat on. Her lips are painted bright red; Ma would be most disapproving.

The mother nods. 'I'm back for a little while.' Then she peers around my sister and looks at me. 'How are you, Cat?'

'I'm very pleased to see you,' I tell her in my finest voice.

She laughs softly reminding me of Dewey. 'Well, that's a relief.'

'Cat's changed, but she's nicer than she was!' Maisy tells her mother.

'She was nice before, Maisy. Come on, leave your sister,' she says in a quiet voice that makes me like her because she's defending Cat.

'Are you two training this morning?'

'We could stay and have breakfast with you instead,' says Maisy sounding hopeful. I know how much Maisy loves swimming so this is a big offer and it must mean she's missed her mother very much.

Mother shakes her head. 'I've been flying all night and I'm very tired, so I'm going to bed now. I'll see you both after school, presents then,' she says.

Maisy reluctantly lets her go, and I have so many questions for my sister, like what sort of mother goes to bed as her children are getting up? And what does she mean by flying?

'I wonder what our presents are,' says Maisy in an excited voice.

'Why would we get presents?' I can't imagine being given presents for no reason. My treasured things at home are in an old tin under my bed. There's a mirror chipped at one side, and a hair slide that Con gave me when I won my first ever race.

'We *always* get presents when Mum's been on a trip!'

'Oh yes, of course,' I lie. I risk a direct question. 'Why did she go away?'

'For work, Cat! Don't give her a hard time. She can't do anything about it.'

The idea of a woman leaving her children and husband to work is very strange indeed, but more thrilling than concerning. I try to imagine explaining this to my sisters, my *real* sisters. Kathleen would mock me and Dewey would laugh. In one way it is unthinkable not to go home—not to find Cat's missing things and trace every clue back to her, and back to my own time. But this simple truth keeps tugging my sleeve: life is so much easier in 2021. There are swimming goggles to protect your eyes, bathing suits that are comfortable and not made of itchy wool and food can be heated in seconds. Not to mention those little teddy biscuits in a packet. I could get used to them.

19

Carnival

No no no no no!

I wasn't meant to fall asleep! The sun is hot on my cheek and the noises of the household tell me everyone else is awake. I was meant to leave for Wylie's Baths at dawn!

Dewey crash-lands on the bed and I turn over to bury my head.

'Fanny, it's race day.'

I reply with the enthusiasm of a cold wet cozzie. 'Ugh.'

'What's wrong? We let you sleep in.'

Dewey touches my shoulder and I shrug her off. As her weight leaves the mattress it reminds me of something: Maisy being nice, me hating it. I don't want to be like that. It's just that I'm always curled up with frustration. I can't believe I've missed the opportunity to sneak away before the race.

'I'll do you some porridge.' Dewey's voice sounds timid. 'Then we'd better head to Coogee.'

I sit up and fling off the covers. 'Coogee?'

'Of course,' she frowns.

'The carnival is in Coogee?' I say, louder, with a massive smile. It can't be too far from Wylie's. Talk about lucky! I can be in the carnival—I have to admit I'm curious—and then try to find the way back home.

Dewey is halfway out the door, giving me a look. 'Will you make the bed?'

I skip clownishly around the room in my nightie, singing, 'Make the bed, make the bed, woo-woo, make the bed!'

'Oh, Fan,' she giggles as she closes the door.

The four girls are ready to go to the carnival. Dewey is entered in a wading race—we do those for fun at school—and Kath and Mary are timekeepers. I wonder about the stopwatch they'll use. I'll have to get a look at it.

Da and the boys aren't allowed to come, and Ma can't spare the time, but everyone says something support-ive when we leave. Frankie gives me his lucky rabbit's foot and I manage not to gag. Next to Dewey he's my favourite. I almost think I could be a good big sister to a funny boy like Frankie.

In my head I say a final goodbye. I don't plan on coming back here.

But the further away we get, the more I can't stop thinking about the money I took last night. In the past I've snitched fifty cents from the bowl of random stuff on our kitchen bench, but that's from my own mum and dad. This is different. In my defence, though, I did it for Fan and her dreams. That makes it a lesser crime, surely. Dewey said something about carnival prizes. Hopefully I'll win some money.

If I win, that is. *Big* if. I don't even know which races I'm in. All this not knowing is tiring. With the number of stupid questions I've asked, the times I've 'forgotten' something, or suddenly become 'distracted' because I don't know what someone's talking about, it's amazing that no one realises I'm not Fanny.

Then again, no matter how strange someone is being, who would ever suspect that they are someone else? I wonder what's happening in *my* life. If Fanny is me, is she doing a good job? She's probably fainted from the shock of everything that's been invented since 1908. I hope she's using deodorant.

We jump on the second tram carriage, where the wooden bench seats face outwards. It's Kath and Mary at either end of the bench, Dewey and me in the middle.

Kath leans forward, holding onto her hat. 'Look at

Fanny.' She winks at Mary. 'That serious face she gets.'

They're making my nerves worse. I've got to find out what's in store for me at this carnival.

'So, there'll be a few races today...' I let the words trail off, hoping that one of the sisters will take the hint and talk about the day and my part in it.

Not one of them says a word.

'I know this is strange, but it really helps me to... *focus*...if someone goes through which races I'm in.'

Mary splutters out a laugh. 'You *know* which races you're in, daft girl.'

'Sure. But it helps when someone else says it out loud. Preparation.' I tap my temple twice. 'Like, "Fan, you've got the 100-metres freestyle first."'

'Metres? You mean *yards*,' Kath says.

Oh dear, how long's a yard? Is it like a backyard? They can be all sort of sizes!

'And what's freestyle?' asks Mary. 'I've never heard of it.'

This is getting worse. No one's invented my best stroke yet! I briefly consider leaping off the moving tram.

Dewey comes to my rescue. 'I'll help you.' She puts on a serious face and does a sort of commentator's voice. 'Fanny Durack, your first race is the 100-yards trudgen, followed by the 50-yards breaststroke, and finished off with the spectacular high dive. I predict you will come first in both races and dazzle the crowds with a dare-devil dive!' She smiles. 'There, how was that?'

I laugh like a nervous horse. Because what on earth is trudgen?

We've arrived at Coogee Aquarium, a huge building with a domed roof that overlooks the beach. I know this place! Mum and Dad took us out for pizza in this exact spot after we'd been for a look at the school when we first moved to Sydney. Spooky.

Inside there's a pool with a tall grandstand on each side. Kath and Mary go off to the judges' area. I want to follow so I can get a look at the stopwatch but Dewey grabs my arm and steers me in the opposite direction. The place is filling up fast with women and girls. I can't believe how many have come. Hundreds! When I race it's only other swimmers' families watching, but these random people have come for fun. I guess this is what people did before Netflix.

I can't lie, I've got excited butterflies as well as a very real sense of dread. The adrenaline is coursing through me and I have to keep shaking out my hands and feet. Lots of people say hello to me and it's a weird feeling, like all the strangers in a shopping centre knowing your name. I think Fanny Durack is a bit famous.

'Hurry, Fan. My wading race is soon,' says Dewey, pulling me towards the changing room. The cozzie I have to put on is navy blue wool. It's loose and long, more like a romper, and the way to put it on is to undo some buttons on one shoulder and step through to the legs. I have a long gown to wear over the top and a baggy cap to keep my hair in place.

I'm getting used to my shape—these strong legs and arms—and I wonder what racing will feel like.

At midday, the first gun goes off and Dewey starts her wading race. The crowd really gets into it, so it feels safe for me to yell out. *'Dew-ey! Dew-ey!'* I can see Kath in the judges' area holding a stopwatch but there's no way for me to get closer.

Dewey comes second and I've literally never seen anyone so happy. I get a wet hug from her afterwards.

'My friend Mabel is in the trudgen race before yours, do you fancy watching?'

'Definitely,' I say, clutching Dewey's arm. She looks surprised but giggles and leads the way. This is perfect. I can see what trudgen looks like before I have to do it myself. On the way, a few girls say hello to me and I just smile and hurry past before they have the chance to chat. I just need to keep my head down during this carnival.

The gun goes off and four girls who look my real age start to swim.

What on earth…? They're doing sidestroke, with scissor legs and freestyle arms, but their heads stay out of the water. I'm going to be so far out of my comfort zone. I've never done that combination in my life!

'Good luck, Fanny. You can do it.'

If only Dewey knew the truth, but it's too late now, the moment is here. It's either get in the water or run out of the building in this strange cozzie. I haven't even warmed up, and I have no idea how to swim in Fan's body. She's taller and stronger and curvier than I am, but my brain only knows how to work my own little self.

Six of us line up; the others look as serious as I feel. A woman wearing a huge hat and a velvet coat with long rows of buttons is in charge. She calls out in a booming voice: 'The 100-yards Trudgen Race!' and we step to the edge. I still don't even know what one yard is, let alone 100!

BANG!

The crowd's cheer melts away as soon as I hit the water. It takes me a few seconds to get the technique but then I find my rhythm. Five heads are bobbing in front of me—this isn't where I like to be in a race. I push harder, but that ruins my technique. I badly want to slip into freestyle but I keep going, scissor-kicking and pumping my arms with all my strength. I have to think about every movement, like when you pat your head and rub your stomach in circles. But Fanny's body is strong and I'm determined not to let her down.

Push, push, push!

The girl on my right stops at the end so I stop too; the race is over. Have I made a fool of myself? What will the sisters think? I climb up the steps, gasping for breath and unable to look at anyone.

'Third place,' says a woman, handing me a round token.

Third?

I came third! That's not bad at all.

As the others wander off I break into a smile. I've been getting first or second place in every race since I was nine years old. But third here and now feels amazing.

After the races, we line up for prizes. The system is that you swap your race token for something—money, I hope! I have my fingers crossed that someone drops a few of those big brown coins in my hand. I got a cramp in the breaststroke race and came fourth, so no prize there. I never get cramp so I feel bad for not looking after this new body I'm in. The trouble is no one has a water bottle, or those nice electrolyte drinks that keep swimmers hydrated.

While we're waiting, I realise I'm close to Kath now.

'*Psst*, can I have a look at that?' I ask, pointing at the stopwatch in her hand. She looks confused but gives it to me. Straightaway I know this isn't the one Dewey used to time Fan at Wylie's, the one I think is now Aunt Rachel's. Yesterday Dewey told me that Mr Wylie's one has something in French written on the clock face. And that's the same as Aunt Rachel's. It said *kilomètres à l'heure*, which I know means kilometres per hour because I do French at Victoria Grammar.

I hand it back to Kath. I need to find Mr Wylie.

'Not as nice as my dad's, is it?' says a girl next to me. It's one of the girls who beat me in the trudgen race. I wonder if she's talking about Mr Wylie. Then her name is called and it's *Mina* Wylie. Perfect! I aim a huge smile at her as if I'm happy for her that she was faster, but really it's because she might help me get the stopwatch.

Here it comes, it's my turn for a prize. A lady with white hair in a bun is coming towards me to present me with...

...*a hairbrush!* This could not be more tragic. Let me get this straight: I broke a hairbrush. So I used someone else's money to buy a new hairbrush. I stole yet more money to replace the money I used to buy the hairbrush. And now I've won a hairbrush!

I wish I could tell someone how funny this is. Tam

back in Orange, Lucy at school, or even my sister—yes, Maisy would love it. All I want is to see Maisy's face in the crowd. To make her smile the way I seem to make Dewey smile. To cheer her in a race the way I cheered for Dewey. I even want to tell her where I hid her yellow Croc.

20

Training

My good mood lasts until we reach the pool. Maisy asks where my goggles are. I tell her a lion ate them and she rolls her eyes and dashes off to see if she can borrow some from lost property.

'Here you go!' She tosses me a bright pink pair. I pull them onto my head and they are so tiny they cut my face in half.

'Oops!' Maisy says laughing.

'Thanks, sister,' I say, moving the goggles down my face so they squash my nose. She giggles, and for a second I can pretend it's Dewey with me.

When we walk into the steamy air, it's my turn to giggle at the sight of Rebecca bent over and contorting her body like a circus performer.

'Never seen anyone stretch before, Cat?' she says sharply and I try to smile. If I have to swim in a relay team with her then it's better for both of us if we get along.

'I'm coming to your party!' I tell her like that should cheer her up.

'Oh, fantastic,' she says in a flat, hard voice.

It makes me wonder why she'd invite me if she doesn't like me. It's all so confusing. In 1908, I don't have time to worry about what someone thinks of me.

'I'm expecting fast times today. You have State coming up and not one of you can take your place in the team for granted,' says a woman rolling towards us in a chair. She moves it with a small lever and she can spin in a tight circle. I've never seen anything like it.

I'm trying to take all her words in. There's State and there's fast. Those words I live for. I can do this.

'In the pool, girls. Start with four laps of breast-stroke,' she says.

The other girls scamper towards the pool. She is the coach. The coach is a *she!* A woman. I couldn't be more delighted.

'Cat!' The woman barks at me.

'Yes?'

'Yes, what?'

'Um…yes, Ma'am?'

Looking baffled, the woman shakes her head. 'It's yes, Coach!'

'Yes, Coach. Sorry, Coach!'

I start taking off my clothes, trying to be as ladylike as I can, but knowing that everybody will see me in this skimpy material and there is little I can do about it. I dive into a lane and try to adjust my goggles so they are not cutting into my face, and then take off after the others. They are miles ahead of me. I'm swimming as hard as I can but Cat's body is just not like mine. I just can't catch up.

This coach is not like Mr Wylie. She yells from the side and times us with a black stopwatch that doesn't look as fancy as Mr Wylie's. Seeing it reminds me I'm supposed to be trying to find the stopwatch Maisy broke and the rest of Cat's things.

Rebecca is much faster than me. She swims at the head of the pack while I trail along behind. From our brief conversation I know that I must usually be faster than her because I'm the fourth swimmer in the relay, so why am I so far behind?

I touch the end of the pool and stand to adjust my goggles and take a breath. This pool is longer than Wylie's and swimming laps at this pace in someone else's body is tiring.

Fingers slam into my back. I spin around.

'What are you doing? You've just messed up the times!' Rebecca snaps at me. 'Don't stop.'

Coach blows her whistle and the other swimmers

glide in behind Rebecca, one at a time. Coach wheels closer to the edge of the pool.

'Coach, I should be swimming the fourth leg. Cat's off,' says Rebecca.

'I'm not,' I say.

'You are,' she says spinning back to me. 'You just caused a traffic jam.'

'Two hundred in your fastest stroke,' barks Coach. 'Rebecca, set pace.'

Rebecca glares at me as she glides away from the wall. The other swimmers follow, but I'm still fiddling with my goggles.

'Where are your proper goggles?' Coach asks.

'I don't know.'

'Maybe Rebecca's right,' Coach says.

'No. I'll show you how fast I can be,' I tell her, knowing that when I swim trudgen I'm fast enough to take Mina.

I push off the wall and start scissor-kicking my legs through the water. My muscles pull in strange places, but I can feel Cat's body starting to speed up. I can't let Rebecca take the fourth spot on the relay.

The whistle cuts across the noise of the swimmers as I touch the end. I look up and see Coach glaring down at me.

'Out, Cat,' she says sharply.

I'm not sure what I've done this time. Behind me the others keep lapping, and I grab my towel and wrap myself up as I walk across to where Coach is waiting.

'What was that?'

Is she asking me honestly? 'My best stroke.'

'Are you joking?'

I shake my head. 'No, I never joke about swimming.'

'Turn around and take a look at the rest of your team,' she says.

The others are all swimming in a stroke I've never seen before. Kicking feet and arms coming out of the water like I do with trudgen but their heads are down and they breathe every third stroke. They're fast too. Much faster than trudgen.

'What possible reason could you have for not swimming freestyle?'

I can't tell her the real reason, so I don't say a word.

Coach pulls a face I've only ever seen when Ma learned I'd snuck out one morning to train when I was supposed to be looking after Dewey and she'd wandered off and no one could find her.

'Trudgen is nobody's best stroke! That's why nobody swims it. It hasn't been swum in at least a hundred years! Can you imagine anyone swimming the trudgen at the Olympics?'

I'm not sure what to say. I dreamed of swimming

trudgen at the Olympics if women were ever allowed to compete. Trudgen *is* my best stroke. Even Mr Wylie says so.

I fight back tears.

'And your breaststroke was no better! Very sloppy. Where's your technique? You're a great swimmer, Cat. Why aren't you taking this seriously?'

I drop my head. I have nothing to say. Mr Wylie is always so encouraging. He never yells at me. I wish I was back in 1908 swimming in my own style, in my own body.

'Do you *want* to swim for Victoria Grammar, Cat?'

I think about the feel of the water moving across my skin. It's as important to me as breathing. I look straight into her eyes. I want her to know I'm serious. I'm not sure how Cat feels about all this, but as long as I'm here, and I'm Cat, then swimming is everything. 'I want to swim all the way to the Olympics,' I tell her.

'Well you won't even be in the team if you keep swimming like you are today. I'm moving you from fourth spot in the relay. Rebecca can swim last leg.'

'I'll swim harder. I promise,' I tell her, furious about the relay.

'Back in the pool. Take your own lane and find your breaststroke rhythm. I want to see your usual speed.'

Relieved I don't have to try to swim freestyle just

yet, I throw the towel into the stand and dive back into the water. I'm going to have to train harder than ever to stay in this team. And until I find Cat's missing things and a way home, I want to do the best I can. Cat might have lost her way with swimming, but to me, it's still everything.

21

Con

As we leave Coogee Aquarium, I spot the path I walked up that morning I skipped training, the one that leads to Wylie's Baths. This could be my chance.

'I'm not coming home with you,' I tell the sisters. 'Bye, Dew.' I pull her into a hug that she doesn't know might mean goodbye forever, and my tummy is fluttering like anything.

'Why, where do you think you're off to?' says Mary. 'Ma will have a list as long as your leg of things to be done by yesterday.'

'I'm going to Wylie's Baths for training. It's important.'

'You can't leave everything to us again,' says Kath.

'I know, and I'm sorry. You just have to believe me— what I'm doing is best for everyone.' I wish I could tell them the real Fan will be back in their lives if my plan comes off.

'I suppose you're going to meet Arthur,' says Mary. 'To give him swimming lessons. Well, Kath and I have been talking and we don't think the swimming association would like it. We're sorry, Fan. You can't take his money.'

This web is getting more tangled. 'I'm not meeting Arthur. I just need to be there,' I say.

'Yes and I need a night out at the Tivoli with a dashing fellow, but I'm not likely to get it,' says Kath. 'We've taken most of the day with the carnival. You can't swim your whole life.'

'Why can't I? Other people do.'

'But not girls like us. With barely two coins to rub together. We're needed at home.'

'But it isn't fair. Isn't there something else you want to do with your lives? Dewey, how about you?'

She shrugs and says, 'Get married and have a baby. I've got it planned.'

'You're thirteen, Dew!'

'And my plan is to be out of Ma's skirts by the time I'm eighteen at the latest.'

'And you two?' I ask the others. They're devoted to organising swimming carnivals, so they must know there's more to life than sweeping a pub floor.

'We can't abandon Ma and Da,' Mary says. 'Da's seventy, John's got his own life. Thomas is god knows where. Con's got a mind to run his own shop. The boys are at school and who knows what they'll get up to.'

'So us girls just get to do the washing and look for a husband?' I reply.

'That's life, Fan.'

If the real Fan were here instead of me would she go along with that? But in this moment I have to be myself, and the thing I'm fighting for is my own life.

'I'm sorry but I don't have a choice.'

I take off up the hill and don't look back, even when they call to me. Arguing with them is the last way I wanted things to end, but the thing I care about most is finding Mr Wylie.

Outside the entrance to Wylie's Baths, I get a feeling like I'm about to sneeze or shiver but I can't. It makes me pause. I'm doing the right thing, aren't I?

Of course I am—I can't feel guilty for wanting this.

There are voices coming from down below where the pool is. It's him, the man Dewey was talking to when this thing first happened—Mr Wylie—and he's down there with Mina. He waves at me as I head for the changing room. The cozzie is still wet but I squirm my way into it.

Mr Wylie and Mina are over the far side. I haven't been in this water since that day and my instinct is to get in and start swimming, see if that's all it takes to get home.

I jump in and squeal—it's freezing, but like always that first plunge makes me feel alive. I dip down and start to swim breaststroke underwater. Maybe, just maybe, when I touch the end of the pool everything will be normal again.

When I think I'm nearly at the end I open my eyes and stretch out my arms to check for the change.

Please work, please make my own hands appear.

Nope. Nothing. No sign of that strange magic.

I can't let myself panic—I've still got my hunch about the stopwatch.

Mr Wylie and Mina are staring down at me. 'Don't be upset about today,' says Mina. 'Father says that with our times we'll both of us make the State team.'

'Oh.' I can't think of anything else to say and I'm scanning Mr Wylie to see if he has the stopwatch.

'Are you quite well?' says Mr Wylie. 'You seem out of sorts. I know you're ambitious and third place isn't what you wanted today. But you can do it. I believe in you.'

'Thanks, Mr Wylie.'

'Now, enjoy,' He gestures to the water and starts to walk away.

'Wait!' I shout, a bit too loud judging by their

expressions. 'I was wondering about your stopwatch. Could I have a look at it?'

'You only borrowed it last week,' says Mina, sounding a little bit huffy. Maybe she doesn't like to share her father's things in case Fan starts to beat her.

'Come now, Mina. But I'm sorry, Fanny, I left it at the house.' By now Mr Wylie is halfway to the stairs and I'm fighting back the tears, realising that I'm stuck here still.

'What's with the face like a sad fish?' says Mina. 'It's only a stopwatch.'

'Then how come you don't want me to have it?' I say.

'First tell me why you want it so much.'

'I just need it. I can't explain.'

'Have your secrets then. But maybe we can think of some arrangement.'

'Like what?'

Mina has a tricky sort of smile as if she's plotting something fun. 'Not sure, I'll let you know!' She skips off after her dad. I'm left in the water with my plan all stuffed up again. Strangely enough there's only one thing I feel like doing. Swimming. There's no one around so I can swim my own way: freestyle.

My session felt good but it's late now and I can't face the Duracks.

I'm hiding across the street in a small park and I can see the pub has been shut up for the night. I've missed supper and must be in a heap of trouble. But I'm scared out here, alone.

Treading lightly, I go through the yard. One of the dunny doors swings open suddenly.

'There you are,' says Frankie, hitching up his trousers to his braces. 'We had bread-and-butter pudding and Ma said I could eat your share, but I said, "No, Ma. It's Fan's favourite." And by the way you're about to see our brother get the belt.'

'The belt? Why?'

'Da reckons Con took some of the takings.'

My stomach flips as I realise he must be talking about the money I stole.

'But he didn't take it, Frankie.'

Frankie shrugs. 'Who did then?'

What have I done? I hitch up my skirt and run up the stairs. In the kitchen, Con has his hands on the table. He flicks me an embarrassed glance. Da's there with a wide leather belt.

'Stop!' I yell. 'It wasn't Con!'

'It's all right, Fan,' says Con.

He's putting on a brave face. But I have to stop this.

'It was me!' I take hold of Da's arm but he won't look at me. He snatches his arm away and tells me to get out.

Where's the kind, jokey Da I know?

'But this is wrong!' I shout.

'Leave it, Fan,' says Con, raising his voice.

So I run out of the room, and as I cry guilty tears in the hallway I can hear the belt striking Con. There is no other sound, not from Da or Con. I can't believe someone as lovely as Da would do that. Or why Con would take it, knowing he's innocent.

If only I hadn't taken those coins.

22

Necklace

My new mother's still asleep when we get home from school and Dad tells us to be quiet and do our homework without waking her. Lucy didn't talk to me all day today. She is really angry about the presentation.

Instead of doing homework, I lie on my bed and try to remember how the other swimmers were swimming. Da paid the entry fee so that I could go in and watch the lessons at Mrs Page's in Coogee when I was nine, but he couldn't afford the lessons. I learned by watching and teaching myself dog paddle and then trudgen and then swimming as much as I could until I was fast enough to compete.

Here in the future I can swim every day if I want to. As much as I miss my family, things are easier for me here. There are more choices. I can go to school instead of having to stay home and help with the chores. I can learn like boys do. I can get a job, eat food from a packet, and wear a thing called a tracksuit.

I doubt Ma would even believe me if I told her what women can do in the future.

Now I need to teach myself freestyle before the next training session or risk being booted off the team. I'm in the bedroom balanced over two tall stools I took from the kitchen. It's a bit wobbly but I start to kick my legs up and down. Then I raise one arm over my head and turn my face to the side under it like they were doing into the water.

I manage my arms okay because that part isn't too different from trudgen, but coordinating my arms, legs and head at the same time seems impossible. Perhaps it's partly because I don't want to un-learn my favourite stroke. If I ever get home, that's how I'll beat Mina.

I roll my head to the side, lose my balance on the stools and crash onto the floor with a yelp.

Maisy runs into the room, shuts the door behind her. 'What are you doing, Cat? You'll wake Mum.'

'Sorry,' I whisper. 'I'm just practising my strokes.'

Maisy glares at me and plonks down on her bed. I jump up and join her, with my knees crossed, impressed at how flexible these joints are.

'Is this because of training this morning?' Maisy gives me a look that suggests she feels sorry for me.

'I'm worried about my place in the team,' I tell her.

'You just need to take it seriously.'

'I do!'

'No you don't,' she says. 'You've relied on the fact that *you're a natural*? I'm sick of hearing it.'

She stretches out her legs. 'I work harder than you. I want it more than you. But you're the *natural*. You could go to the Olympics if you want to. I'm just not sure you do.'

'I do. Believe me. That's all I want.'

'You have a funny way of showing it, Cat.'

I've always been lucky that my sisters are happy for me to be the swimmer while they pursue more ladylike things. It's obviously not the way with Maisy and Cat.

'Mum's up,' says Maisy, as the door to the other bedroom creaks open. Barely containing her excitement, she jumps up and leaves.

I carefully balance myself across the stools again in an effort to try to work out this stroke. I have to be able to swim it at the race meet on the weekend. If I don't then I'll be off the team.

We've eaten fancy pastries for breakfast, and now my new mother, whom I'm struggling to call Mum, hands me a beautifully wrapped box. Maisy is ripping the paper open on her present, but I go slow, not wanting to ruin the corners or the edges or the folds. I lift up the flap at the end and slide out a small blue box.

Inside is a gold necklace with a pendant that has a swimmer lifting her arm as she glides across the water engraved on it.

'What a treasure!'

Maisy and my mother laugh. 'See! I told you she was different,' says Maisy.

I look up at them both grinning at me and I grin back. Mum takes the box from me and tells me to turn so she can fasten it around my neck. I go to lift my hair up to help her, and then remember that I'm not Fanny and I have short hair.

The only necklace I've ever had was one that I won in a race, and it was nothing as fine as this. I feel the pendant against my neck, reminding me I'm a swimmer.

Maisy has a swimming necklace too but hers is silver. Like second place I think to myself, while mine is the gold of first. I wonder if Maisy had the same thought.

I have so many questions for my new mother. About where she's been and what she's seen and what she does with her time. 'Are you always away for so long?' I ask, amazed that mothers can leave their families.

'She wasn't on holidays, Cat! She was working,' snaps Maisy. 'You always do this. Make her feel bad for being away. It's her job.'

Mum squeezes Maisy's hand like she's calming her. 'I don't think Cat was suggesting I was swanning around Europe.' She turns back to me and sips from a cup of tea. She drinks it black like Ma does, but this is made from a teabag and this mother leaves the bag in.

'It was long this time. But Paris was lovely. We were only there a night but I did get to see the Eiffel Tower.'

I nod but I have no idea what she is referring to. Luckily Maisy dives in with chatter about French food and snails. I listen, trying to pick up as many scraps of information as I can. There is something about flying and business class and serving people in the air and I gather that the aeroplane I saw my first day here is where she works. She delivers meals, like a servant in the sky. The idea that a plane can hold so many people and that someone can walk around in it is hurting my head.

'Tell me more about your travels,' I say, wanting details of lands I've never imagined. My family always marvelled if we ventured as far as the mountains for a day on the train.

Mum looks at me and I see how blue her eyes are. They are nothing like Ma's dark Irish eyes. This mother looks more like Maisy than like Cat. She's strong and slim and I wonder if she was ever a swimmer too.

'London was busy and we didn't have long before we

had to fly out. I went to some galleries in Paris and ate stinky cheese!'

I laugh. 'Like cheese left on the bench too long? Cheese on the turn?'

Mum tilts her head like she's examining me and I realise I've spoken strangely again, like someone from another time. I push my chair back to escape her close watch. 'I might start on dinner if that's okay? I'm starved.'

'See?' says Maisy to Mum. 'She cooks now. Told you she's weird!'

23

Names

Being someone else feels different now, like a pair of new runners that are starting to remember the shape of my feet. For days I've been picturing the look on Con's face when Da belted him. That happened *because of me*—Cat. I made the choice to take the money and Con got punished.

It's made me think about the kind of person Fanny is. All the clues I have are from the way people talk to me. She must be kind and funny, and ambitious. I don't think she'd let the strict rules for girls in 1908 stop her from doing anything. I get that from the way Mr Wylie and Mina were talking, all the fretting out loud Ma does, the sisters saying there are no choices for girls, as well as a gut feeling.

It's teatime. The meal is delicious tonight: potato puffs made from yesterday's meat mashed up with boiled potatoes, then flattened into saucer-sized rounds, dusted in flour and fried in boiling fat. There's also pickled red cabbage and a loaf of bread that Mary baked. The whole family is at the table, except for Ma who hardly ever sits down. If Ma isn't feeding us she's feeding the stove with wood, or clearing out the ashes, or chucking out the kitchen slops, or preparing the next meal. Kath and Mary are always bobbing up and down from the table to help her. The boys have their chores but they get to sit and enjoy the meal.

'I said, any more for you, Fanny?' says Ma. 'Can somebody nudge that girl?'

'Sorry, Ma,' I reply. 'I was thinking about something else.'

'Her race on Saturday, I'll bet,' says Con, smiling.

Frankie says, 'She'll win for sure this time,' and then he and Mick start chanting, *'Fann-y! Fann-y! Fann-y!'*

They're so sweet but I can't help cringing: I've almost got used to plain Fan but every time someone calls out *Fanny!* I squirm as much as if they were yelling *bum* or *boobs*. I know it's just old-fashioned, but come on!

Then I get a brainwave, and I'm going to try it the next time that someone calls me Fanny.

'Pass the butter, Fanny,' says Dewey, literally a second later.

'Actually,' I begin. 'I've decided I want to be called Franny from now on.'

Nobody moves or speaks. Then I feel Dewey take the butter dish from my hand and the entire family bursts out laughing. They think I'm joking!

'I mean it!' I try again. 'I think Franny sounds better.'

They just keep laughing, except John, who is shaking his head. I got the idea from Mum. She was reading *The Magic Faraway Tree* to Maisy and me, but when she got to a character called Frannie she frowned and left the room. Maisy and I got out of bed and followed her into the den, which had these giant storage cupboards that Dad built. Mum was rummaging in there for ages and finally found what she was looking for—her old copy, from when she was a kid, with her name in biro on the browned pages. 'See?' she said, 'In my day that character was called Fanny. They must have changed it for a modern audience. I wish they hadn't.' But we talked about how children today might get the giggles when they heard the name Fanny.

'You're a card, Fanny,' says Da. A *card*? I think it means I'm hilarious.

'Never mind all of this nonsense,' says Ma, 'what I'd like to know is where young Frankie's shoe is.' Everyone turns their attention to Frankie, who looks guilty. We all look under the table. Frankie is wearing only one brown boot.

'Well, Ma, it's a funny story,' he says cheerfully. 'You see I was going down Foveaux Street coming home from school, just minding my business, you know, and this fella who's nearly finished building a brand new house he says, "Would you mind giving me your shoe?" and I says, "What do you want my shoe for?" and this fella says, "I'm about to brick up the last wall and we need a small shoe for luck—as it happens yours is the perfect size." So I gave it to him.'

'You did what!' shouts Ma. 'That's your only pair of shoes! What have you to say about this, Tommy?' She nudges Da, and I'm terrified that Frankie's going to get the belt.

But Da raises his cup of tea at Frank. 'That's my boy. Wards off evil spirits, a boot in the wall. It's good luck he chose yours.'

Ma huffs and goes back to the stove. 'Ridiculous. Good luck, indeed. We can't afford good luck.'

No one dares to say another word after that, but everyone is smiling again. I get a rush of love for them; they're not just someone else's family, they're *my* Duracks too. Now I feel bad for what I tried to do with the Franny thing. Her name is Sarah Francis Durack, Fanny or Fan for short. And if she's in my place like I'm in hers, I don't want her changing things either.

My main plan hasn't changed—I'm going to track

down Mina Wylie and get that stopwatch. But while I'm here I'll do whatever I can to win a race for Fan.

24

Stopwatch

If I were home in the pub, we'd all be up by now with a list of chores as long as my arm. But it would seem that here sleeping until mid-morning on a Sunday is almost expected. Lying in bed while I wait for someone else to wake up I've had time to think about everything that has happened to me in this future place.

As much as it is tiring to pretend to be someone else each day, and not to have an ally like I do with Dewey, I think I'm growing to understand Cat a little more. And I can't help but wonder if she is being me, how she has fitted into my life.

A buzzing noise breaks my thoughts and Maisy groans from her side of the room. She reaches across and grabs her phone. She tosses it to me.

It lands near me. 'I don't want it!' I tell her, picking it up like it's a live grenade.

'Answer it. She'll just keep calling!' Maisy snaps.

I don't know how to answer it, so I hold it up near my face. 'Hello?'

But the phone keeps on buzzing. Maisy glares at me. 'What are you doing, Cat?'

Relieved when the phone goes quiet, I toss it back.

There's another buzz and this time Maisy presses something before she throws it across. I squeak at the sight of the girl's face trapped in the small screen.

'Cat! Finally,' she says.

This girl is talking through the phone at me. I can see her blinking eyes and long red hair. There's a ring through her nose. The poor thing.

'I've left about a million messages, Cat. What is going on?'

'Um...' I try to think of what to say. 'I lost my phone.'

She sighs deeply. 'I knew it.'

I'm trying to think of a way to ask who she is, and what she knows about Cat, but I'm finding it very disconcerting that she's staring at me.

'How are you?' I finally say.

She frowns. 'Yeah, you know. Sammy and I broke up. Again! I should have listened to you,' she says.

'I'm so sorry.'

She pulls a face. 'You hate Sammy. Why would you be sorry?'

It's hard to have a conversation when I don't know who I'm talking to or what I'm talking about. 'I'm sorry for you,' I say.

The girl on the screen starts laughing. 'You're being odd this morning, Cat!'

'I am. It's true. Why don't I call you when I find my phone?'

'Oh, okay. I thought we could catch up. It's been ages! I miss you. We all miss you. Or have you traded us all in?'

Now I laugh. 'No! I miss my old friends too,' I say, being as honest as I can. 'You have nothing to fear. I will never belong here.'

I manage to say goodbye to the girl and the phone goes black.

'Tam and Sammy broke up again? Those two,' says Maisy, sitting up.

Tam. Now I know the girl's name. Maisy suddenly looks across at me with wide eyes. 'Sorry, I shouldn't have listened in.'

'Why? I'm using your phone and we share a room,' I say, thinking of how little is private in 1908.

'You're doing that *weird* thing again. Maybe we should try to find your phone?'

'About that...I'm pretty sure I left it at Wylie's Baths. I went swimming there.'

'When?'

I'm not sure if I should tell Maisy that's why Cat skipped training. I shrug.

'When did you go the baths, Cat? Did you go alone?'

Even if I wanted to answer Maisy's questions, I can't. So, I say the one thing I know will distract her. 'We could go now if you like?'

Maisy swings her legs around and looks across the gap at me like she's trying to work something out. 'You want me to come with you?'

'If you're not busy.'

The smile Maisy gives me reminds me of when I invite Dewey somewhere. Now I'm pleased that I asked her to come, wondering if perhaps I could tell her the whole truth.

Today I'm sure is sunnier than it ever is in 1908. We make our way down the path to Wylie's Baths.

'I'm glad we brought our bathing suits,' I say.

'Since when do you call cozzies bathing suits?'

I'm too excited about visiting Wylie's to be concentrating on pretending to be Cat. This time there is no sign or roped-off entrance. They must have completed the work on the wall because the turnstile is open.

'I didn't bring money,' I say.

Maisy groans. 'Here, but you owe me,' she says,

pulling a note from her pocket. It's blue and shiny and nothing like the heavy coins we have in 1908. I wish I could keep it and take it back to show Dewey.

The boy at the counter takes our note and we head through. There are a few people swimming already and I can feel a pull in my body as we head down the stairs.

'Why did you come here when you can swim in a pool?' Maisy asks. 'Isn't the bottom all slimy? Are there fish swimming around?'

I laugh at the horrified expression on her face. 'Yes, but it's magical,' I tell her.

Maisy snorts. 'Magical! You never talk about magic!'

'You're right,' I say, pulling her by the arm to the smooth rocky area under the stairs. 'But maybe now I do.'

I scan the area trying to think where Cat might have left her things. I know there was no bag in the changing room that day so maybe she took it down to the rocks with her. That would make sense: she had fancy thing-ummybobs in her bag so she'd want to keep it in sight.

'I believe that I left my bag somewhere around here,' I say. 'You look that way and I'll go over here.'

There are no men in little pants today. I duck down and wedge up under the rocks to where I'm hoping I'll find Cat's bag. But there's nothing but orange peel and a pair of cracked goggles.

'Cat!' Maisy calls. She's holding up a backpack and grinning like she just discovered gold.

'You found it!'

Maisy hurries over. She watches as I open the bag and pull things out. Everything is damp. I hand a flat green parcel with something hard inside it to Maisy because I'm looking for the stopwatch.

'Cat, this is wet. It's been rained on. I bet your laptop is dead!'

'Dead? What do you mean?' Horrified I shake it, hoping to bring life back.

'Maybe we can dry it out in some rice. Isn't that what you do with phones?'

I have no idea what she's talking about. How does rice dry things? I go back to searching the bag, my fingers brushing against squashed sandwiches that smell bad and empty plastic packets.

'No stopwatch,' I tell Maisy. 'Maybe she dropped it.'

'*She*? Who were you with? Lucy?'

Shoving everything back into Cat's backpack, I ignore Maisy as she blathers on about the missing stopwatch and what Aunt Rachel will say. All I can think about now is that I might never make it back home. I will be stuck here with dead laptops and other things I do not understand.

'Do you know her?' Maisy says.

I spin around and see the leathery lady from that day. She's waving as she swims towards the steps of the baths and pulls herself out. Her swimmers seem even smaller than when I last saw them.

'I've been waiting for you. I have something of yours.'

She takes something from her bag and walks towards us. My heart is speeding up at the thought that maybe she found the stopwatch. As she holds it out to me, I see a solid silver case that's not as shiny as I was expecting. But then I spy the watch face with its circles of different numbers, and the words in French and a long thin timer hand. It's Mr Wylie's, has to be.

'You found it.' I throw my arms around her in an impulsive hug.

'I had it fixed for you,' she says with a smile once I've let her go. 'My granddaughter happens to be a very good horologist.'

'Thank you,' I say, wondering what that means. Maisy gushes over the repaired watch, talking about how happy she is that Aunt Rachel's eBay antique isn't lost.

'I'm so pleased, girls,' the lady says as she walks away. 'Take care now.'

I turn the watch over in my hands. 'What do you think has been fixed?'

'The hand of course. The button was stiff and when I finally pressed it the timer hand started spinning backwards.'

I think of the whispering words I heard at the pool. *The hand unwinds.* I wonder if it was Cat telling me that the hand of the stopwatch had unwound time. Maybe she's stuck there waiting for me to unwind the hand and switch places with her again. But how do I do that? I need to know how the watch was fixed.

I look around to ask the lady what her granddaughter did to it, but I can't see her. She's not in the water. Her bag has gone too. She's vanished.

Now that I have the stopwatch, I ache for my home. But if I don't know what was done to the watch to fix it, how will I use it to unwind time again?

'Can't believe how lucky you are getting all your stuff back. Come on, let's swim. It's baking,' says Maisy, undressing by the rocks.

I wish a simple swim could fix my problems. Watching Maisy, and weighing the silver watch in my hand, I can think of one person who might be able to help me figure this out.

25

Confession

For once I wake up before Dewey. I lift my head to see Kath and Mary but their bed is already made. My brain starts to whir with thoughts about the stopwatch. If I get my hands on it, what will I need to do next? I remember how dizzy and strange I felt watching the timer hand unwind, so do I need to make it spin extra fast and clockwise to travel forward to my own time?

I can't know for sure if the real Fanny is being me but that's what I suspect. She was at Wylie's, I was at Wylie's, and so was the stopwatch. I just hope she noticed it on the rocks where I left it and also thinks that it's the link between us. It's no good not having a theory—I've grabbed one and I'm sticking with it until I'm proved wrong. That's what Lucy would say and she's the most scientific person I know.

Dewey murmurs in her sleep. We're lying very close and I breathe in the smell of her hair—if I'm honest, she smells like a cup of tea. We use leftovers from the teapot to wash our hair. I've been using salt to scrub my teeth and they're furry as a cat. For a minute I let myself imagine the sharp taste of toothpaste. Long, hot showers. Dad's lasagne. Mum's arms around me.

Nope, got to stay strong.

'Hey, sleepyhead.' I sit up and gently shake Dewey.

'My tummy,' she moans. 'I must be on the rag, can you get the belt for me?'

What can she mean? She can't mean Da's belt that he used to whip Con the other night. I climb over her as she groans again and draws her knees up. I think I know what it is. Her period! Facing away from her, I press my hand on my tummy through the nightie, panicking that if Dewey's got her period, I'll get it too. Mum told me that sometimes when girls live together they have their periods at the same time. In my own life, I haven't started yet.

'Never mind, I'll get it myself,' Dewey says, throwing off the covers. She pushes past me, grumpier than I've ever seen her. After rummaging in the drawers she pulls out a strappy looking thing and what looks like old napkins. What a nightmare. This is another reason to get home as fast as possible. But I feel bad for Dewey.

'Do you mind, Fan? Some privacy?'

'Sure. I'll make you a hot drink. And sneak a bit of Ma's fruitcake for you.'

'For breakfast?' she says, but looks as if she loves the idea. Her face is back to normal: soft and smiling. Mum always has chocolate when she's got hers, so why not fruitcake?

Later, as Dewey is 'on the rag', she sits at the table peeling potatoes and I'm on ironing duty. Luckily I've watched Kath do it so I don't have to ask for instructions.

To iron a sheet, I lie it on the kitchen table over an old blanket. Then, on the kitchen range, I heat two irons that are more like my dad's 10-kg weights. To test if they're hot enough, I lick my finger and touch it—'*psh*'—on the iron—very safe, *not*. The handle gets roasting too, so a cloth has to be wrapped around it. I have to keep the range going, use one iron while the other is heating, and keep swapping them. It is *hell*.

After this I'm supposed to make bubble and squeak from Sunday's leftover veg. Everything we eat is stodgy. I never thought I could miss salad. Chores are my whole life now. I'm really over today.

'What's wrong, Fan?' says Frankie, coming in from a game of laneway cricket. 'You look like you're chewing a wasp.'

'Just bored,' I tell him.

'I bet you'd just love a swim,' he says, and he sounds so sweet, as if he'd dig me my own personal swimming pool if he could.

I put the iron back on the range with a loud clang. 'I *need* a swim. I can feel it all over,' I say, but there's no chance of that. I sink onto a stool at the other end of the table and rest my head for a while as Frankie and Dewey start a food fight with the potato peelings.

'Sarah Francis Durack! *What* am I to do with you?' Ma yells as she bursts in. 'The fire's gone out *again*!'

'I'm sorry, Ma! I'm no good at being stuck inside all day.'

'Oh, is that it? Then I've got the perfect job for you, my girl. You can collect the chamberpots from the bedrooms and empty them down the back.'

'Please no, I'll be sick!' I plead. But there's no getting around Ma.

Now I'm walking down the stairs with a large bowl of dark yellow wee in each hand. Please don't let me trip on my skirt. Please don't let any of the strangers' wee touch me.

I make it down safely and get rid of the wee down the drain, trying not to splash my boots.

Con's in the yard smoking a roll-up.

'What did you do to deserve that?' he says, with a smile.

I've been wanting to speak to him about the trouble I caused him. 'Con, I have a confession.'

'Shall I fetch Father Robert?' he jokes.

I shake my head. 'It *was* me who took that money. I wish I'd tried harder to make Da believe me. I'm literally so, so sorry.'

'*Literally*?' he raises his eyebrows.

'I'm being serious, Con.'

He flicks the cigarette butt across the yard. 'I know it was you,' he says quietly.

'How? And why didn't you dob?'

'What's *dob*?'

'I mean, why didn't you tell Da it was me? Why let him hit you?'

'I saw you that night sneaking down to the bar. But I couldn't very well let him hit *you*, Fan.'

'You mean because I'm a girl.'

'Well, that and all the times you've been kind to me, sis. We're family. It's what we do.'

I swallow a lump, half-thinking that I want to pay Con back but also wishing I could click my heels and be with my own family: to be honest with Mum about the flatness I was feeling every time I thought about training and the way that the scholarship was like a whirlpool I'd been sucked into, and why I was so cranky at everyone. Especially Maisy.

Suddenly there's shouting coming from the bar— much angrier than the usual shouts of daytime drinkers.

Con is off like a shot—I put the chamberpots down and follow him.

On the way we hear a gunshot and breaking glass.

'Keep back, Fan!' Con hisses, but I stay with him. He's creeping cautiously and we duck down low as we reach the back entrance to the bar.

We can hear Da saying, 'Don't do anything rash,' and then, 'Stay calm, lad.'

Con crawls on all fours and I'm right behind him, doing the same. We inch along silently, hidden from sight but with a view of half the bar. The pub has cleared. I can hear Con's tense breathing.

'Just give me the bloody money!' It's a man's voice, hoarse and slurring. I can see the back of Da's head and his hands in the air.

I take off my boot, tap Con on the shoulder, and mime throwing the boot into the far corner. He nods and gets ready.

With all my strength I hurl the boot. It hits a framed picture dead on and the glass cracks before the boot drops to the floorboards.

There's another gunshot, a man's roar and a dull thump on the ground.

Da shouts, 'Hold 'im down, Con!'

I peek out from behind the bar. Con's on top of a man and Da's on the ground holding his legs. The gun is out of reach but the man is struggling.

'Fan! Get the police!' Con shouts through the strain of keeping the gunman from escaping.

'How?' I say, not caring how stupid I sound.

'Stick your head out the door and yell, darlin',' Da says with a wink.

I yank the pub door wide.

'Police!' I yell as loud as I can over the noise of trams and horses. I wave my arms, standing there in one boot. 'Help! Police! There's a gunman in here!'

A few people start to run away from the pub, but up the hill I hear some voices repeating my cries for help. Some street kids first, and then finally some adults. There's a loud whistle and I see two tall men in dark uniforms and caps running this way.

'In here,' I shout.

The gunman struggles and Da and Con put all their weight on him, grunting.

The policemen rush in and take over. Con helps Da up, and Da pulls him into one of those man-hugs with a slap on the back. He keeps his hand on Con's shoulder and they grin at each other, and although I'll never forget Da whipping Con the other night—or my part in it—I feel something like relief that I was part of this. I finally did something I'm proud of. And the strange thing is, even though I'm still Fan, I've never felt more like me.

26

Lucy

There was a tricky moment this morning when Dad asked me to check something on my phone and I couldn't. Maisy answered for me, pretending that she beat me to it, because he doesn't know yet that both my phone and laptop are 'dead'. They are both now hidden under my bed, in a large baking tray and covered with white rice.

I still haven't managed to work out how to unwind the hand of the stopwatch and the only joy I've had this morning is the takeaway bacon roll Dad made me for breakfast that I am three large, messy bites into. I've never tasted anything so delicious. I can't believe food all ready to eat can be purchased like this so quickly without having to make it at home.

'Are you going to tell Dad about your stuff?' Maisy asks as we head into school.

'I hope I don't have to,' I say.

Maisy shakes her head. 'You can't hide it forever.'

I grin at her to change the subject, aware that I have bits of bacon stuck in my teeth. She groans and looks away, as Lucy darts across our path and heads into the school building in front of us.

'Didn't Lucy see you?' Maisy says.

'She's probably got her head in a new experiment. I need to catch up with her. Bye, Maisy,' I say.

Lucy hasn't spoken to me since the great presentation disaster. I catch up with her at our lockers.

'I'm not talking to you,' says Lucy before I've said a word.

'Lucy, wait. I'm sorry about the presentation. I'm not feeling myself lately. My head is jumbled and I'm getting everything wrong.'

She fixes her mouth, tight, like she's trying to work out a response. 'I've never heard you apologise like that before.'

'Oh. But I'm sorry. Really, really sorry.'

'Well, I'm sorry too. I'm just super-stressed about keeping my scholarship and the presentation was worth a lot of marks.'

'I'd give you all my marks, if I had any.'

She nods. 'You know what, you're being...*different*, Cat. More human, less exercise machine. And what's with the bacon roll?'

'Dad bought it because I was starving after training.'

'First spag bol and now this. You never eat bacon. You're all happy-pig obsessed. And you're a vegetarian!'

'That was last month.'

'Have you hit your head lately? Perhaps it's amnesia,' she says, and she's being serious. 'You could have a concussion.'

'I'm fine,' I tell her. The more suspicious she becomes, the more afraid I am about someone in this time finally knowing the truth.

'But you said you're not yourself. And there must be a reason. There is always a reason.'

She leans in and studies my face for what feels like ages. 'You and I have been greeting each other the same way every morning since we became friends, and for the fifth time in a row you haven't used that greeting. So come on, Cat, what is our greeting?'

'Um…' I try and think but all I have are the insults that Mina and I toss around jokingly, like the ones we trade about each other swimming like our legs are tied together.

'Cat, seriously. That's proof, right there that something's wrong. If I wasn't a scientist and I didn't know that it was impossible, I would say you actually are a different person.'

I step back and smile. 'Nope. Same old Cat!'

'I'm not convinced. I might have to run a few more tests.'

I imagine myself strung up in a laboratory with wires coming out of me, and I shudder. 'What sort of tests?'

'What did I say to you on the first day we met?'

Perhaps experimenting on my body would be preferable to testing a memory I don't have. 'Umm. Good morning?'

'Wrong. I told you a joke about a giraffe and you laughed.'

'Oh yes, of course. I remember.'

'Try this one. What is on my bedroom wall?'

'A painting?'

She nods. 'Of?'

'Flowers...'

Lucy is frowning hard. I've seen that expression in science class. 'It's true. You can't be Cat. Cat gave me an Einstein poster as a present for Christmas. If you are not her then all my belief in science is being tested. And I'm on the verge of a career that will lead me to great things. You're confusing me, Cat-not-Cat! We need to get some help on this.'

She turns sharply from me and starts to scurry down the corridor towards the science rooms. I hurry after her.

'I love proving theories,' she says, hugging her bag. 'But if I prove that you are not Cat…that is terrifying, perplexing and scientifically impossible!' She whispers the last point as if just confirming this to herself.

'Would that be so bad?' I say.

Her eyes widen. 'What are you saying?'

I want to tell her, but the worry in her eyes tells me that she is not ready to hear it.

'Lucy, all this time I've just been practising acting. So I can audition for the part of Juliet. Of course I'm Cat. Who else would I be?' I say it as lightly and flippantly as I can.

'So you're pretending not to have a memory. All this time.'

'And my nerves are strained. I mean, I'm super-stressed. Like you. About swimming and whether I'll be on the state team. I've just been moved from swimming fourth leg in relay, Luce.' I hope that distracts her.

'Oh, Cat, that's awful. I'm sorry. Look, testing my hypothesis that you are not yourself has been flawed with a faulty source. That means you. Of course you're really Cat, because anything else is unscientific and who else would you be? But I think you need to see a doctor.'

I thought I could tell Lucy who I really am, and ask

for her help to get me home, but she's so scientific that she'll never accept it without proof. And where am I going to find that?

27

Dewey

On Thursday we crawl into bed after midnight. Con had to give a statement at the police station and John had a date (we teased him a lot) so as the next strongest I helped Da with the beer barrels. Now, even my bones are tired.

'Blow out the candle,' I say, stretching out on cool sheets.

Dewey gets in close and says, 'Good night, sleep tight...' She squeezes me and says, 'You say the rest.'

Half-asleep, I mumble, 'Don't let the bed bugs bite.'

My dreams are strange and a voice pokes me awake when it's still dark. But there's no sign that it came from one of the sisters. The voice said: *how to unwind?* And now I think about it, it was Fan's voice—the one I've been speaking all this time. But does that mean the words came from the real Fanny Durack, wherever she is? I chew on the words with my sleepy brain.

The next time I wake, I open my eyes and take a gulp of air as if I'd been held underwater. There's a weight beside me, making the covers tight. Dewey is sitting there, staring.

'What is it?' I ask in sleepy confusion.

'Look me in the eye and tell me the truth.'

'What's going on?'

'That's what I want to know.'

At first I think that Con's dobbed about the money, but then I get a chill from the look she's giving me.

With a shake in her voice she says, 'What's happening to you?'

I'm about to make a joke out of it but I'm tired of the lie. A big part of me wants Dewey to know who I really am.

I push myself up so we're face to face.

'I...you see...sorry, I'll start again. Everything's fine, but...my name is Cat. I'm from the future.'

She springs off the bed and turns away from me. She whispers prayers and paces to the door and back. I'm scared—what's going to happen now?

'Do you hate me, Dew? Are you going to tell?'

'Tell? They'll take you to the madhouse if you say such things! Fan, you're not well.' She's crying and I'm scared the rest of the family will hear.

'Dewey, please. You're the one who asked. You know

something's happened.'

'But it can't be true,' she sobs. 'The future? You can't be someone else.'

'It *is* true. Think back to the clues. Please, I'm begging you.'

Looking unsure, she sits on the bed again. 'Well…it was silly things at first. All your forgetfulness. Doing things as if you didn't know how. You were even in the kitchen holding the bellows the wrong way round and blowing air into your face.'

I remember that and almost laugh, but she looks so serious, I bite the inside of my cheek.

'And last week I found a note in your purse. *Hi, I'm Cat, I was you…*' She bursts into fresh tears, pressing her face into her hands. 'Why didn't you tell me?'

I touch her shoulder.

Dewey peers out of her hands. 'I thought you had a disease of the mind, but then this idea crept up on me that…that…'

'That I wasn't really Fan.'

'Don't say it! I had to go to Father Robert to confess unnatural thoughts!'

'What did he say?'

'He told me to say fifteen "Our Fathers" and stop being a silly chit. And I did my penance, I tried to make the thoughts go away but last night you said the wrong words. *Good night, sleep tight...*'

She searches my face for the rest, but I can only shrug. 'It isn't the line about bed bugs?'

She shakes her head. 'You have always, always said, *wake bright.*' She cries a bit more and then dries her face. In a weird moment of calm, she stares at me. 'It's really not you, is it? I can see it now, in your eyes.'

'I'm really not Fan, that's true. But these are her eyes, not mine.'

'The saying goes *The eyes are the window to the soul.* You're you, I suppose. You can't be anyone else, including my sister.' Dewey gets up, as if she's horrified all over again, and heads for the door. I scramble ahead of her and block the way.

'Please don't tell everyone.'

'Tell me where she is!'

I try to take her hand but she snatches it away.

'Dewey, please. I can't know for sure but I think your sister is in my life, being me. Don't tell. We can fix this together.'

A noise outside the door makes us both hold our breath to listen. There's nothing more but Dewey lowers her voice.

'Where is she?'

'It's not where, it's *when.*'

Dewey's bottom lip quivers.

'I need to take you to Crown Street. Get dressed,' I say.

'But I've got school.'

'Well, haven't you ever wagged before?'

We tell Ma I'm walking Dewey to school. Ma is curious about Dewey's red face but I whisper about Dewey being 'on the rag' and Ma nods.

It's silent between us, up the steep hill. Ten minutes later we're outside *Ernest Ireland, Pastry Chef.* Home—sort of.

'Dewey, this is where I live. Only not in 1908. My life is more than a hundred years from now.'

Her eyes expand like ink dropped into water.

'I don't know for sure but I think Fanny is there. As in, I'm here in her life, and she's in the future in mine.'

Dewey gasps.

'I didn't make it happen, I swear. It was when I was swimming at Wylie's Baths—that day when you timed Fan with the stopwatch.'

'I remember! You broke my hairbrush. You were angry and a little unkind. Not like my sister.'

'Yeah, that's me. Back home I have a reputation for being angry with little sisters.'

Dewey checks the windows above the shop awning.

'So she's there, but *not* there. If I believed you—and I'm not saying I do—it sounds so far away.'

'I know, but coming to the past hardly took any time at all.'

'So, it happened when you were swimming. Are you a proper swimmer like Fan?'

'Yes. Even though I was wagging training.' I shrug.

'And then all of a sudden you were her and she was you?'

'Well, I was her. I'm guessing the rest. I know I sound like her and look like her, but all my thoughts are mine. It's been so lonely.' I want to add *apart from having you*, but I'm too shy.

She takes a deep, shuddery breath. 'So I can't go in there now and get her,' she says, in a way that shows she already knows the answer.

Dewey and I walk around the city, going over the last two weeks. She buys a currant bun because we haven't eaten, and as she hands half to me it feels like a sign that we could be friends.

We find a park and sit on a bench by a sapling. I wonder how big it is in my time. A huge tree, probably.

'What'll it be like for my sister, in your life?'

'Amazing. Different. There's more of everything— people, traffic, food, bright lights, and *stuff*—there's so much *stuff*. It's hard to explain. There are inventions that make everything faster. You can talk to people a thousand miles away on a telephone you carry in your pocket. You can listen to music whenever you like on the phone too. The food! Dew, the food is incredible. And girls wear whatever they like. Girls can *do* anything. It'd literally blow your mind. Australia has had a female prime minister. And of course most people have two heads.'

'What?'

'That last bit was a joke. Just trying to make you smile, Dewey.'

But it's too soon for Dewey to see the funny side and I can't blame her for that.

'Is Fanny ever coming back?' she says.

I'd like to tell her how scared I am about this. Dewey and I are the same age, but here and now I'm supposed to be the big sister.

'Definitely. We'll make it happen at Wylie's.' I smile, trying to look confident. 'Everything will go back to normal soon. Right now Fanny will be eating like a queen, hanging out with my sister Maisy and my friend Lucy, and swimming in the amazing pool at my school. My family is great, Dew, I wish you could meet them. I share a bedroom with Maisy. She's kind, funny, works hard. She *can* be annoying, and she never has any trouble getting out of bed in the morning.'

Finally Dewey smiles. 'Not like you.'

'No. So, I have to know—are you going to tell?'

She shakes her head, and wipes currant-bun crumbs from her mouth. 'The shock'd *kill* Da. Ma would string you up and beat you till you dropped right out of Fanny, and then she'd insist we go to church every single day till the end of time. No, I'll keep the secret. I love my sister—and from what you say she'll be having the time of her life in the future. I know I would be. There aren't many adventures for us. You've seen how it is. And if she's being you she'll be looking after things, you can count on that.'

We walk back the way we came, exchanging a few shy smiles like new friends.

'Can you really keep my secret?' I ask.

She spits on her hand and holds it out.

'That's gross, Dew.'

'Fanny'd shake my hand.'

So of course I have to.

'Thanks, Dew. You're awesome.'

'I'm what?' she says.

'It means really, really great.'

As we walk I tell her about Netflix, space travel, ice-cream sandwiches, YouTube, tampons and bras. I don't tell her about the wars—the First World War is only six years from now. Her brothers might have to fight, even Mick and Frankie. I'd hate to know if terrible things were about to happen in my time. And after all, Dewey can't stop anything. All anyone can do is live the life they've got. Including me.

On Saturday I wake to an empty room. I can hear and smell heavy rain outside—the window is propped open with a chunk of driftwood. I lean over and put my face in the gap, watching the downpour—the shiny backs of horses trotting past and the sludgy street, black umbrellas like beetles.

It's race day. Last night, with Dewey's help, I practised trudgen on the rug between the two beds while she sat on the bed, laughing at me. I described bikinis to her and she didn't believe me, so I rolled up and pinned Fanny's underwear into a bikini shape, and made her do the same. Then we pretended we were walking down to the beach (the rug), to lie in the sun (the gas lamp) and apply sun lotion (Kath's jar of cold cream). We were laughing so much that Mary and Kath came in and their shocked faces made us howl even more.

Just like she promised with the gross hand-spit-shake, Dewey doesn't give me away.

I walk into the kitchen and find Ma, Kath and Mary eating breakfast.

'Where's Dewey?' I ask, cutting a wonky slab from the loaf of bread.

'I've not seen her,' says Ma.

Mary shrugs, 'Nor I. She'll be out the back with her friends I shouldn't wonder.' The laneway is where a lot of the kids hang out.

'How are you feeling about Brisbane, Fan?' asks Kath.

'What?'

'Honestly, she's still half-asleep,' Mary laughs. 'The State Championships? Kath's got her eye on a new hat for the occasion.'

Kath's eyes sparkle. 'A chaperone has to look her best, sister.'

I shove bread into my mouth as an excuse not to have this conversation. After I've washed it down with lukewarm tea, I offer to sweep the backyard to make up for another mammoth sleep-in. The yard door has been left open and it sounds like a playground out in the laneway, so I put my head out. There's a game of cricket in play, with kids of all sizes.

I yell out to Mick, who's fielding a long way down the lane. 'Hey, Mick! Where's Dewey?'

He returns a dramatic shrug just as a ball cracks against the bat and comes soaring his way. It lands neatly in Mick's hands and there's a big cheer as kids stampede in his direction.

I grab Frankie's sleeve as he runs past. 'Frank, where's Dew?'

'Haven't seen her since last night.'

No one's seen her. This is so strange.

She wouldn't, would she?

But she would, wouldn't she...

I have to tell more white lies so I can find Dewey without raising suspicion.

While Kath and Mary are distracted by chores, I yell out, 'Taking Dewey for a swim, see you at the carnival at noon!' And I run outside. I can't believe I say *noon* now.

Back to the serious business of finding Dewey.

I take the tram to Wylie's Baths. It's still pouring as I go down the steps to the pool. The ocean is churning, with a moody sky above it. Mr Wylie is walking swiftly alongside the pool as Dewey swims a messy breaststroke, dipping her head under and then coming back up for a gasp of air.

I know why she's here—she's trying to follow Fanny into my time.

When I reach Mr Wylie, holding onto my hat as the wind and rain lash my face, Mina appears in a long black swimming cloak.

'She's been swimming up and down for hours, Fan.

What's got into her?'

'She's just training.'

'She's exhausted,' says Mr Wylie.

I feel so guilty. Maybe Dewey was trying to reach her sister, or maybe she wanted an adventure of her own because of everything I told her. But hundreds of people swim at Wylie's every week—they don't all slip through time. I still don't know why it happened to Fan and me. I don't even know if we really have swapped. For all I know, my brain devoured hers. Just ate it up! It does sort of sound like something I would do—by accident, of course.

Mr Wylie turns to me. 'Fish her out, will you? I don't like the look of those waves coming over the edge.' And then he leaves.

'Need a hand?' says Mina.

'Thanks but I've got this. Mina, about the stopwatch.'

'You wanted another turn with it. How about a bet to make this afternoon's carnival more interesting? If you beat me, it's yours for a week.'

'Breaststroke then.' I spit into my palm and hold it out.

Mina doesn't hesitate. 'Deal,' we say at the same time. I like Mina; she's fun. But I really hope she has a terrible race.

When she leaves I hurry to the end of the pool to

grab Dewey as she finishes another lap.

'Dewey! I'm so sorry!'

She stops swimming and stays low in the water, breathing hard. Her eyes look sore and sad. This is my fault—I told her about everything good in my time. I haven't told her about refugees, climate change, extinct creatures, plastic in the ocean.

'It didn't work for me because you and Fanny are special and I'm not.' She's shivering and crying and my heart hurts for her.

Then the rain stops. I look at the sky to see a rainbow arching above the ocean. 'Dew, it's a sign.'

'Of what?' she says grumpily, but she looks where I'm pointing.

'I told you how much we know in the future about science and stuff, right? Well, if you see a rainbow above an ocean, the science says you're going to meet an adventurous boy and see the world.'

She bursts out laughing. 'That's a load of codswallop.'

'You never know. Come on, time to go.' I hold out my hand, and this time she takes it.

It takes ages to get from Coogee to the carnival in Drummoyne. We just make it in time. It's packed again—women and girls only. Like Wylie's, it's a pool cut out of solid rock.

Now that Dewey knows I'm really Cat, I can whisper things that I had to keep to myself before.

'Better find Mina,' I say, 'and make sure the deal is still on.'

Dewey grabs my hand as I'm leaving. 'Good luck.' She smiles but I can tell that she's still upset about this morning.

Just before the race, Mina shows me that she's brought the stopwatch with her. It's exactly the same as Aunt Rachel's. For a second I'm tempted to snatch it and run, but no more impulsive plans. I'm pumped to race, knowing that when I had Aunt Rachel's stopwatch with me at Wylie's—and the timer hand was winding back so fast it made me dizzy—Dewey was timing Fan with it. Same watch, same place.

The gun fires and we're off. I just go for it with the breaststroke technique Coach taught us. At first I feel awkward and I'm losing heart. But then I find some more fight. By halfway I feel longer and stronger with each stroke. And I'm not aware of the girls either side of me, which might mean...could it mean...have I...

Yes! I've won!

Mina doesn't make me wait.

'*That* was impressive,' she says when we're drying off.

When I take it from her hand, mine is still shaking from the adrenaline. And it hits me that what I'm happy about is that I had a goal I believed in and that made me so fast. This is even better than a medal. I can't wait to show Dewey.

It's nine o'clock and dark by the time we get home by tram. Dewey hugged me the whole way.

From the street I can see that the light is on upstairs in the kitchen. I know that Ma will be in there, keeping the fire going. Frankie and Mick will be in bed. John will be in the parlour reading the paper. Con will be laughing with the men in the pub and Da will be lifting beer barrels or chucking out drunks.

It makes me think of life back home. About Maisy and how things are between us. She trains harder than me, follows the rules. She wants to swim more than anything and I treat her like a pesky fly. I've enjoyed being the one on top. But now I'm not exactly sure why. I'm the one with the box of medals. Maisy's the one with the passion.

What does it mean if you're not passionate about the thing you're really good at?

I'm lying in bed now with a strange feeling. Even after winning today, I don't know if I'm meant to be a swimmer.

28
Party

Tonight, Mum ate three serves of my lamb stew. I couldn't help but feel a little proud that she liked it so much. Maisy grumbled about me no longer being vegetarian but then tried the stew and devoured it too. Apparently, Cat likes something called tofu, which sounds like a sort of disease.

Now Maisy's washing up and Dad's drying and I'm lying in Cat's comfortable bed while Mum perches on the edge of Maisy's. I am beginning to understand why Cat doesn't like getting up in the morning. If I slept in a bed this soft, I probably wouldn't either.

'How's everything going, Cat?'

'I'm going to Rebecca's party tonight.'

'Rebecca from the relay team? I didn't know you were friends.'

Ma and Da know most things about my life back home. They know about Mina and her father. They know that I live to swim, and that I secretly love Dewey the best. I wonder what Cat's mother knows about her.

'I don't think we are,' I say. 'I'm not going to the party because of her. I'm going because it's a party and apparently they can be fun.'

She laughs like she understands. 'Have you heard from the girls?'

'Girls?'

'Your friends in Orange?'

'Just Tam,' I tell her, still marvelling over the idea that someone's face can appear inside a phone.

'Are you feeling better about us moving here?'

I've wondered about this from little things Maisy's said about Cat not wanting to move. In my time my parents just make decisions. I can't imagine anyone asking me what I think.

'At least we didn't move all the way from Ireland,' I say thinking of Ma and Da moving across the world for a better life.

'Why would we move you from Ireland?'

'It was in a book I was reading.' I avoid her eyes, worried that she'll know I'm spinning yarns.

But she nods. 'Ah, was it a cookbook? Is that why we ate Irish stew for dinner? I did wonder.'

Of course. Da always says Ma's stew reminds him of home. 'I'm trying the meals eaten by Irish people around the beginning of the twentieth century,' I tell her. 'For history class.'

'Right. Does that mean I'll find rabbit on my plate soon?'

I nod. 'If I can source one that seems fresh enough.'

Mum starts laughing. 'Maisy will explode if you feed her rabbit. Remember Bunny?'

I nod confidently like when Ma asks me a question about the washing and I don't remember her instructions.

'I have to fly out on Monday so I'm not going to see you race next week,' says Mum. 'I'm sorry.'

I'm used to my parents not seeing me race. It's a rare day that Ma comes along, and Da isn't allowed.

'Do you have to fly for long?'

'A short haul to Tokyo and back,' she says. 'I'd love to take you two there. Maybe we can think about going to the Olympics to watch the swimming,' she says. 'That's if you haven't already made the team in a few months,' she says smiling.

'Watch the Olympics?' I ask. 'Really?'

'Why not? We can save up, and my job helps with the flights.'

'We could see the Australian team? The women?' My voice is too eager. I try to contain the bubbling feeling in my stomach, but the thought is thrilling. Perhaps I could stay here a little longer. There's no way I'll ever have an opportunity like this back home.

'I'll talk to Dad,' she says. 'Might spur you on a bit!'

'I don't need spurring on. I'm going to swim at the Olympics one day if it's the last thing I do.'

Maybe I shouldn't be in such a hurry to make the hand of the stopwatch unwind again. Would I be wrong to enjoy a little more of Cat's time?

I'm not sure what tonight's party will be like. I'm imagining some dancing and some games. Cat's wardrobe is full of tiny clothes that look more like they're made for a doll than a person, but I try them on because I can hardly wear my school uniform to a party.

The first top exposes more of my middle than my bathing suit does. I know it's not actually *my* belly but even Cat's belly deserves more material than this little floral thing that I currently have on. I try a longer top that reaches my knees and, with long pants on, there is very little skin to be seen.

I'm beginning to understand the appeal of not having to run a hairbrush through my long locks every night. This hair needs nothing but the odd wash with sweet berry shampoo.

I haven't experimented with any make-up as Cat and I'm not sure if she wears any. Back home I would have had Kathleen help with some colour on my cheeks perhaps, but here I don't know what to do.

'You're wearing that?' Maisy barges in with a face.

'Yes?'

'To a party?'

I nod, looking back at myself in the mirror, and letting doubts creep into my head.

'A nightie?'

I look down at the pale blue fabric and realise it's not a top at all, but something you wear to bed.

'And those pants are Mum's old ones. No,' says Maisy, pulling at the nightie and checking me out. 'Or is it fancy dress?'

'I don't think so.'

'Rebecca lives on the hill, Cat. You need to look good.'

'So help me, will you?'

Maisy does that thing she does with her eyebrow when she can't quite believe how incompetent I am, and then gets busy in the wardrobe. Clothes are thrown wildly in my direction.

A bright pink blouse hits me in the head, and I giggle. 'I can't wear everything!'

'I'm looking for that black lacy top. You know, the one Mum bought you for the Grade Six formal?…Here it is.' Maisy holds it out to me and I realise that you can see straight through it!

'I can't wear that! In public!'

Maisy starts to laugh. 'It's better than a nightie!'

'But…you can…see…' I hold it up in front of my face and look through at her.

'That's the whole point! It looks nice on you. Just wear a crop top under it if you don't want to just wear a bra.'

What is a crop top? It's all so confusing.

'Here!' Maisy thrusts a tiny singlet at me.

Maisy turns around so that I can get changed. I strip off, not caring that she's in the room. I get undressed in front of my sisters all the time. It's funny that people in the future are so keen to show skin to strangers but not to people in their family.

I pull the singlet on and then slip the lace top over and peep around Maisy so I can see myself in the mirror.

'Looks good,' says Maisy, fiddling with my top so that it hangs better. 'Not those pants though.'

I let her return to the wardrobe while I stare at myself in the mirror. I know I'm not me to look at, but I'm me on the inside and there is something so freeing about wearing clothes that let you move without corsets and layers pinching skin and covering every tiny patch of your body.

I wouldn't even wear this to bed in 1908, and now I'm about to wear this to a party. I grin at my reflection and it grins back.

Mum is driving me to the party because Rebecca lives in Bellevue Hill and Mum says she can't resist having a look. She says millionaires live there. I don't think I've ever seen one but I suppose millionaires just look like normal people.

'Nervous, Cat?'

'It's the same feeling I get before a race,' I tell her.

Mum smiles and grabs my hand. She gives it a squeeze. 'I never think of you as getting nervous. You always seem fearless.'

Maybe that's what Cat and I have in common. Both swimmers, both fearless. This churning feeling is excitement. It *is* the same feeling I get before a race, but it's not nerves.

'It won't be that different to Tam's party. Just a bigger house,' says Mum, as she pulls up outside a very large, very grand white house built into the side of a hill. 'A *much* bigger house!' she says, laughing.

I whistle and Mum laughs. 'I've never been in a house like this,' I tell her, and then I panic because I don't know if that's true for Cat.

'Do you want me to come in with you?'

I shake my head, knowing that Cat would definitely not want that. I have no idea about how she would react to some things, but for others it's very clear.

'Thanks for driving me.'

'Call me when you want me to come and pick you up.'

'My phone is at Lucy's,' I lie. It's even harder lying to Mum than to Maisy.

'Then I'll be back at ten. Can you survive that long?'

I grin at her. 'I think so!'

The sounds of the party float down to me as I get out of the car and wave Mum off. I straighten my top and start walking up the very steep hill. I think of Dewey and how impressed she'd be by this house.

The garden smells sweet and clean and I suck as much of the air in as I can. My Sydney smells like horse poo and dirt.

Some boys rush up behind me laughing and bundle past before I can move for them. One bangs into my arm.

'Oi!' I yell after him, pretending that it's my brother Con and some of his friends. I miss their roughness and their noise.

I reach the top. From here I can see the harbour and I search for Lavender Bay Baths, hoping it's out there somewhere and hasn't been pulled down like so many things from my time.

'You came, Cat!'

'Well, you invited me.'

Rebecca is standing at the door wearing a very small white dress. It's as tight as a bathing suit and as short as a top. Her hair is even longer than my real hair and it's out and wild.

The house is even grander than I'd imagined. Chandeliers of glass beads hang from the ceiling. I stare at the walls of paintings and at the staircase that sweeps upwards. It's covered by laughing, chatting people I vaguely recognise from Cat's school.

'It's so grand,' I tell her.

Rebecca laughs and the sound is cold. 'Grand? What are you, a hundred? Drinks are in there. Toilet's through there. Enjoy,' she says, turning dramatically on her toe and heading into the crowd.

There must be over a hundred people here. That's a lot of friends. In 1908 I have rivals who are sort of my friends, but only because we swim together.

I decide to go looking for cake. But the first door I open leads to a room of people dancing and flashing coloured lights. Nobody seems to care about how their bodies are moving and I'm so intrigued that I step into the room to watch. There are boys jumping up and down in a circle in the oddest way I've ever seen. I spy a small group of girls from the swim team. They are all dancing different sorts of moves at the same time and there is obviously no routine to learn so, without thinking too much, I join them.

Everyone around me is bouncing up and down so I start stepping from one side to the other, swinging my arms and twisting my body. I've won prizes for dancing, but here in the future I can't quite keep up.

I decide to close my eyes and enjoy the music. Someone bumps me. It's a girl called Taylor from the swim team. 'Sorry, Cat!'

Taylor is moving her hips in ways I didn't know possible. I try to copy her but I'm wooden and stiff and I can't work it out.

'Teach me?' I yell over the music, feeling bolder now.

'Sure!' she says, and she turns so she's in front of me and I can mirror her. I start trying to swivel through my hips, sending them from one side to the other. Soon I'm dancing more like Taylor and it's marvellous. As the song finishes, she grins at me and holds up a hand. I'm not sure what she wants me to do.

She looks at me strangely. 'High five?'

'What?'

Taylor lifts my hand up and taps it against hers and I realise I'm supposed to slap palms with her.

'Oh! Sorry. Now I get it,' I say, holding up my hand. Laughing, she high fives me.

'You're different tonight,' she yells over the music.

'Really?'

'Not such a snob,' she says.

From what I've learned about Cat, she may be rude and grumpy and sometimes not nice to Maisy, but I don't think she's a snob.

'I'm just a bit shy sometimes,' I tell her, wondering if that's true.

'Really? But you never talk to any of us. Rebecca said it's because you think you're better than us because you're on a scholarship. '

'I don't think I'm better than you. Well, maybe I'm faster in the pool!' I say lightly, hoping she gets my joke.

'Not when you swim that weird stroke,' she says laughing.

I smile. 'My turn to teach you a dance.'

I start dancing the way I do at home, tapping out the rhythm of the tune with my feet and stomping on the ground with my arms held high. Soon the two of us are clearing a space in the room, with everyone else around the outside. Some of the boys start cheering and as the song finishes Taylor grabs my hand and pulls me down into a bow. I feel flushed and hot, but happier than I've felt in days.

I leave Taylor and keep looking for cake. I find a large

table bursting with food in the front room of the house where it's quieter. I stare at a plate of what looks like raw pink flesh. A boy walks up and grabs a sandwich.

'Excuse me, do you know what this is?' I ask.

'Sashimi,' he says.

'What a beautiful word!'

He laughs and grabs another sandwich. 'Sounds better than raw fish!'

'Really? Is that what it is? Raw fish?'

He nods. 'Haven't you seen it before?'

I shake my head. 'No. Where I come from we don't eat raw fish.'

'Where you come from? You mean Bathurst?' says Rebecca, who has suddenly appeared beside me.

'Orange,' I tell her.

She laughs. 'Yes of course. Orange! Where all the great swimmers come from.'

The boy shrugs at me like he's apologising for Rebecca, and then he grabs two sandwiches and leaves.

'By the way, thanks for swimming so strangely the other day. Now I've got the fourth leg of the relay.'

'Congratulations,' I reply, heeding Ma's advice to be polite.

'Better watch your scholarship. They'll take it off you if you keep swimming like that. Then you'll have to go back to Bathurst.'

'Orange.'

'Whatever.'

In 1908 we're competitive, but we are never mean. We might be disappointed if we are beaten, but we are also happy for each other when one of us wins because in a way it's a win for all of us. We are all trying to change things: to get paid in prize money not trinkets, to swim in front of everyone, not just women, to be able to aim for the Olympics without fearing that the rules will never include us.

'Why are you being so mean?' I blurt out, knowing Ma would understand my rudeness.

'Mean? I'm not. I'm just pointing out that I'm going to take you down, Cat. You might have been a good swimmer in Orange, but I'm the best swimmer at Victoria Grammar.'

I'm so stumped by her words that I really don't know what to say. I realise the room has gone quiet and that others are listening. My cheeks are burning and I'm furious for Cat. This girl with her big house and her even bigger hair has no manners. I just wish I could swim freestyle well enough to beat her.

'Thank you for inviting me. I had a lovely time. Good night,' I tell her, holding in all my ugly thoughts for when I'm outside.

As I head out I pass the large platter of cakes with

little butterflies made out of chocolate on top. I take one for later, and then grab another for Maisy, and walk as slowly and calmly as I can towards the door.

Lucy was right. I don't like Rebecca at all. If I do end up staying longer in Cat's time, I won't spend another second with her.

29

Beach

Someone's banging pots in the kitchen. Da calls out, 'Rise and shine, Duracks!' and I think that's Ma laughing. I've never heard her laugh. We sit up in bed and give each other *what's-happening?* looks.

When the family is gathered at the kitchen table, Da and Ma stand at one end looking like they've won the lottery. Da pretends to play a wooden spoon like a bugle. Ma shoves him.

'Stop that, you daft old man.'

'Sorry, my love. Now then, attention, Duracks! I do declare that on this very day, the something of March 1908—'

'Fifth, Da!' yells Frankie.

'Thank you, my boy—the fifth of March 1908—that we, the Duracks of the Newmarket Public House, Sydney, New South Wales—'

'Tommy, get on with it!' Ma giggles.

'Are having a grand day out!'

The whole table erupts. Even John smiles and he's usually about as much fun as a potato! Dewey's grin warms me up like porridge.

'Where are we going, Da?' says Con.

Da tries to play the spoon bugle again but he doesn't get very far—Ma's laughing like a seagull and wiping her eyes as she says, 'We're going to the beach. I've packed a picnic.'

Everyone but me jumps to their feet and starts to dance around the table. Maisy and I didn't even react like that when Mum and Dad took us to Bali. I'm so happy for them. A whole day to swim and laze around. But I had my own plans today, to take the stopwatch to Wylie's and try to get home.

'Which beach are we going to?' I ask over the noise, crossing my fingers they say Coogee.

'Bondi, of course,' says Da.

'But first!' Ma roars to get our attention. And then in a gentle voice she says, 'Church.'

There's a bit of a groan and we race back to our rooms to get dressed.

We walk to church in twos like the girls in a book I loved when I was little, about a girl called Madeline. In front of Dewey and me, Frankie and Mick are boasting about the height of waves at Bondi. 'Taller than the pub,'

Mick says. Wide-eyed, Frankie asks him if he thinks he can swim in waves like that, and Mick says, 'Sure, no problem,' but I can hear a wobble in his voice. It's not as if anyone in the family has had swimming lessons. Dewey told me that Fan taught herself when she was ten.

I've only seen Bondi Beach in photos before now—I can't believe I had to travel back in time over a hundred years to come here for real. Squad training is so full-on that my days boomerang between home and school. There and back, like swimming laps.

But here we are.

It's baking hot with a warm wind that's making all the girls hold onto our hats. The beach is packed but I can hear the waves fizzing on the shore and I can't wait to be in that sparkling water. Not far off there's a group of teenage girls paddling but they won't get far in what they're wearing. Their cozzies are navy blue belted dresses with a white or red trim, worn over pants with frills at the knee.

Frankie and Mick run ahead and find some space for us. They do backflips in the sand until we catch up. I can do those in my real body but there's no chance in these uptight clothes.

'Can we go exploring?' asks Frankie, out of breath, arm around Mick.

'I should think so,' says Da.

'What about my picnic?' Ma exclaims. She's laid a white tablecloth on the sand and she's pinning it down with ginger-beer bottles.

'Let them run free,' Da replies. 'Go on, boys.' They've gone in a flash, flicking up the sand with their bare feet. 'Now, what about you lot?' he asks us older ones.

'We'll have a dip first, shall we?' says Kath. 'Let's go up to the sheds to get changed.'

Ma sucks in air and tuts. It's because of my swimming costume—the one made of thick wool that goes halfway down my legs. Ma calls it *impure*.

'It's fine, Ma,' I say.

'In front of every Tom, Dick and Harry,' she replies grimly. I think her laughing inner-seagull has died. She's all flustered, taking things out of her basket and putting them back in as if she can't decide whether to lay out the picnic or go home.

'Dewey and I swim every weekend in those costumes at carnivals.' I remind her.

'But there are men here,' says John like the fun-time potato he is.

Now even Da looks unsure. 'Maybe John's got a point.' He narrows his eyes at the beach crowds. 'It's not sending the right message, showing yourself like that, Fan.'

'But it's not safe to swim in a dress. The water gets inside and drags you down. I'm a swimmer and my costume is the best thing to swim in. It's that simple.'

'I agree with Fan,' says Dewey.

'See, she's corrupting Dewey,' says John.

Con mutters under his breath and then he claps his hands loudly. 'John, you're looking a bit hot there.' He lunges at his brother, lifting him onto his shoulder as if he weighs nothing! Da laughs his head off as Con charges at the water and dumps John in the waves.

Ma gasps, 'Poor John, he won't like that!' At last she's smiling again.

Da grabs Ma in a bear hug and kisses her face roughly. 'Don't fret, woman. Let them have some fun.' He winks at us four girls and, to the sound of John shouting at Con, we head to a ramshackle building to get changed.

'Was it okay that I talked to Ma like that?' I whisper to Dewey.

'You said the words Fan's said to me many times,' she smiles. 'Only, I'm not sure she'd have said them to Ma and Da.'

'Oh…sorry.'

'Don't be! She wanted to say them, it's just she felt like it was her against the world sometimes, you know?'

I think I do.

•

Us four girls sit in the shallow surf. Dewey and I are in tight woollen costumes—at first I felt embarrassed when we got some disapproving looks, but the haters need to get a life. It's just arms and legs. If they don't like it, they should look away.

What Mary and Kath are wearing looks more like a dress—long with puffed sleeves. They've both got their hair stuffed into blue shower caps. Hardly anyone else is in a swimming costume—most people just have their shoes off. Some of the teenage boys are in costumes like ours. The rest of the men have rolled up their trouser legs. It's strange to think that I'm probably the best swimmer on this whole beach. There are little kids playing in the shallow waves, and not many going further out, which is good because there's a dark, flat patch of water out there that might be a rip.

'Look at our brother,' says Dewey, pointing at John. He's standing like a dripping wet lamppost next to Ma's picnic, staring out to the ocean.

'Poor John,' says Mary. 'Born without a funny bone.'

'Meanwhile, what about Con,' says Kath.

Con's got five girls standing around him, gazing up at him like they're madly in love.

'Can you imagine if that was me standing there for all the world to see with five young men?' she says.

'Ma'd have you to the nunnery,' giggles Mary.

'I don't think there's much chance of admirers while you're wearing that swimming cap,' says Dewey.

At that, Kath picks up a mass of seaweed and puts it on top of her cap so it streams down like hair. We shriek with laughter as she keeps a perfectly straight face and pretends to look confused by our reaction, adding more seaweed, smoothing it down and fluttering her eyelashes. I pick some up and do the same, and the others follow. It's all over Mary's face. And it stinks! We roll around in the water, laughing and trying to hold the seaweed in place.

'Fan, here comes your friend,' whispers Kath.

I look behind me and shield my eyes from the sun. Who does she mean? I'll look stupid if I can't find my own friend. Is it Mina? Or one of the other girls I've swum against like Dorothy and Gladys, who are impossible to beat at trudgen. But I don't recognise any of the girls on this beach.

Then I see Arthur. The boy who recited poetry and gave me his handkerchief, which I stuffed into Fanny's bedside drawer and never thought of again. The boy everyone thinks I've been giving swimming lessons, for money! It looks like he's with his family: mum, dad and two little sisters. And they're heading straight for Ma and Da.

I pull the seaweed off my head and hurry towards them.

Ma spots us and rushes over with some long robes, which she makes us put on before we come any closer. 'The Gon family have come to say hello,' she says, looking flustered. 'Isn't that nice?'

Arthur smiles, tilting his cap back. I do a little curtsy for some unknown reason. Being in 1908 is doing strange things to me.

'Father, Mother,' he says. 'May I present Miss Fanny Durack. This is my father, Mr John Chung Gon, and my mother, Mrs Mabel Gon.

'Ah, the swimmer!' says Arthur's dad. He's a smartly dressed tall Asian man, and on his arm is a short curvy white woman with one of the biggest hats I've ever seen.

'That's right,' says Da. 'All my children can swim, but none so good as Fan.'

'Of course, your Arthur would know that,' says Ma, 'taking lessons with my daughter as he does.'

I start coughing as violently as possible to create a diversion. I bend over for more drama. Dewey smacks my back. 'Sorry!' I croak, and keep coughing. How long do I have to cough before everyone forgets that Ma just said I've been giving Arthur swimming lessons?

Suddenly there's frantic yelling and we all look in the direction of the water. A crowd has gathered at the water's edge.

'There's a boy out too far,' shouts a blonde woman,

breaking free of the group.

I see a bobbing head, way out in the water, just a dot.

And I realise who it is when Mick comes tearing up the sand towards us even before he shouts, 'Frankie's out there!'

'Oh, sweet Jesus,' cries Ma.

I sprint to the water. Con is struggling to take off his shirt, but he's not a strong swimmer. If he goes out there, he could drown too. I search for the lifesavers in yellow and red who patrol the beaches in my own time, but there's no one like that with a board or a dinghy to rescue Frankie. Everyone's shouting and Ma is screaming her lungs out for someone to help her boy. His head keeps disappearing, then it bobs up again.

'They're running to get the lifesaving reel,' says Mary. I don't know what that is but we're wasting time.

'Fanny!' says Kath, tears streaming down her face.

Dewey grips my arm. 'Fanny's done the training,' she whispers in a desperate voice that no one else can hear.

I drop the robe and start running. I'm already deep enough to dive in and swim.

Am I really doing this?

Yes. I'm meant to, I know it. I've never felt such strength. I'm Fanny Durack and that's my brother Frankie out there.

I'm not scared. I'm the best swimmer on this beach and I'm going to save him.

I can't get my rhythm. It's different in the waves. The water is fighting me every stroke. Each time I look up I'm not where I expect to be. I can still see Frankie but I can't hear voices on the beach any more. We're alone.

Frankie is thrashing when I get to him, reaching up one arm and then the other as if he's climbing an invisible ladder. His eyes are wild with panic and he can't see me.

All my training has been in a pool. I try to get hold of him but his body is slick with saltwater and he keeps pushing me under.

Then I remember: *help from behind.* I take a huge breath and dive under, swim behind Frankie and hook him underneath both arms as I kick hard to the surface.

He's lies still against me, but he's light and I'm getting my breath back. 'It's okay, Frankie!' I gasp. 'I've got you.' He's not moving at all. It's easier to hold him but I wish he'd say something. His eyes are closed.

I stay in place, treading water, with his head tipped back on my shoulder. And I take long breaths, looking up at the sky, my eyes and throat stinging.

'I'm going to carry you to the beach, Frankie.' I try to sound sure of myself.

His head lies heavily on me and the water laps against his pale chest.

'You rest. I can do this.'

I can't see his face properly or tell if he's breathing.

I start to swim with rescue-backstroke legs, holding him tight. When I risk a backward glance at the beach it looks like we haven't moved and I want to cry.

No, I tell myself. I can do this.

'Keep going!' I yell. 'We've got this, Frankie!' He's so slippery and the waves keep battering us. I'm trying to ignore how tired I am, but it would be so easy to give up. Part of me thinks that if I don't let go of him, he'll drag us both under.

All of a sudden I feel an arm go under my chin and I scream.

'I've got you,' says a deep voice. 'We're on the line. They'll pull us back in. All you have to do is lean on me.'

'He's not breathing,' I shout, still kicking my legs.

'Stay calm and still now. Let the line do the work.'

It feels wrong to stop swimming, trusting this person whose face I can't even see, but then I feel us being dragged through the water. So I hold myself still, hold Frankie tight and focus on the sky.

It's over, and I'm alive. But what about Frankie? I whisper in his ear, 'Please wake up.'

In a whir of people and voices, finally we're on the sand.

'We need a doctor!' a man yells.

I'm kneeling by Frankie and there's a crowd around us. There's foam at Frankie's mouth and his chest isn't moving. I think that person screaming is Ma, but I'm not quite connected to the moment, dazed and out of breath.

Mr Gon pushes his way to the front with Arthur. 'My son is studying to be a doctor,' he says.

'There must be someone else,' says another man, not even looking at Arthur and his dad. I think back to that argument in the kitchen and I know it's because they're Chinese.

'Arthur can do it! Please!' I shout.

'Please, son,' cries Da. 'Help my boy.'

The crowd gasps and jostles to watch as Arthur kneels at Frankie's other side.

Da, Con and John hold them back with their arms outstretched to give Arthur room.

Arthur starts the kind of compressions we learnt in Health class, firm and even. He tilts Frankie's head back to breathe into his mouth. More compressions. Hard, but steady. I hear a bone crack and the people behind me gasp.

One of the men yells, 'Get the boy a real doctor!' and he yanks Arthur's shoulder.

Da grabs the man by the front of his shirt. 'Touch

him again and you'll deal with me,' he says fiercely.

Arthur is back to the compressions, looking calm and sure.

'A broken rib can heal. Let me continue,' he says.

When he next breathes into Frankie's mouth, I see the little body convulse. Arthur turns him onto his side and a stream of foamy water comes out of Frankie's mouth. He heaves and retches and coughs. Arthur strokes his back firmly and says, 'Good boy. You're all right, Frankie.'

After that, an older man pushes his way forward and says he's a doctor. Somehow the crowd swallows Arthur up and I can't see him anymore.

30

Protest

Walking down the corridor, I hear, 'Hey, Cat' more than once. I smile as I walk past faces I recognise. I could belong here.

As I get closer to my locker there's a group of girls beneath a sign that reads: *Dorothy Hill Was a Geologist. And a Woman!*

Could it be my Dorothy Hill? The Dorothy that Mina and I are always trying to beat? But how did she become a geologist when in 1908 she's a swimmer like me? I don't even know what a geologist is.

It's then that I hear Lucy's voice, loud and clear and angry: 'Women can be scientists too!'

I push through the group to get to where Lucy stands in her white lab coat and big beautiful combed-out hair, waving her sign.

Lucy sees me and lunges forward. 'Cat, they told me to apply for the special science program over the summer, but *all* the places have already been filled with the boys from Merkham Grammar. There isn't a single place for me, or any other girl. It's so sexist!'

'Oh no,' I say. 'Is there anything you can do?'

The first bell goes and the others start to flutter away, leaving just Lucy and me in the corridor.

'I worked so hard on my application. I really want it, Cat.'

'So fight for it.'

'That's what I'm doing!' she says, waving her banner.

'I mean not just in school. You could go to the press.'

She giggles, and it's such a lovely, light sound. *'The press*? You mean newspapers?'

I nod. 'Yes. My friend Annette Kellerman did it…I mean, I read about her once. On the Google.' I think of Annette's defiant expression on page one as she stood in the bathing suit that got her arrested in America.

'On the Google?' Lucy giggles again. 'And who's thingy Kellerman?'

'Annette Kellerman. A swimmer from a long time ago.'

'Did it work?'

'It must have done. She was arguing for the right to wear a swimming costume.' People swim in bathing suits tinier than anything Annette Kellerman could have ever dreamed of. And nobody cares. 'So that's what I'd do, Lucy. Tell your story and get the public on your side.'

Lucy stands straighter as if her mind is churning with ideas.

'I have to do something. Because if I can't be a scientist, I'll die.'

'I know,' I tell her. 'But you will be a scientist. You already are one. You just have to get them to understand that you are the best possible person for that program.'

She nods. 'You're right. I am a scientist. And I am going to get in.' She grabs my shoulders and holds them tight. I can feel her passion for the life she wants pumping through her, like her body is tingling at the idea of fighting for something.

'Can I ask you something, Lucy? Who is this Dorothy Hill on your sign? Was she a swimmer?'

Lucy laughs. 'No! She was a geologist and palaeontologist. Born in 1907. She was the first female university professor in Australia and a scholarship kid like us. She became a world expert on fossil corals and people still use her research today.'

Born in 1907. So she's not *my* Dorothy.

'Ancient, I know,' says Lucy. 'But she changed the world.'

'Not that ancient,' I say, my voice sharp with a feeling I can't explain to Lucy.

'I just meant, *imagine* what she would have had to battle back then so she could be a geologist. If she did it, so can I.' Lucy leans her sign up against the lockers.

As she gets her books for class, I wonder if *my* Dorothy Hill ever became famous. I wonder about Mina Wylie, too. Most of all I wonder about myself. If I stay here, I'll never know what Sarah Frances Durack could have been. If Cat is living my life, as I've imagined ever since I heard the words *the hand unwinds* in the swimming pool, will she fight for women to swim at the Olympics the way Mina and I have talked about? And would I want Cat to do that, when it's *my* fight?

I pull Lucy into the fiercest hug, trying to transfer all my fight into her. 'I know what it's like to have people telling you that you can't do something. It's up to us to make them let us.'

She pulls away, giving me a strange look. 'You've never been one for inspirational speeches, Cat, but thanks. Now come on, we have to get to class. Protesting is fine, but not if I have detention.'

At lunch, I pull Lucy to a quiet spot on the grass near the art buildings. Talking to her this morning about Annette Kellerman, I realised I have an urge to tell her who I am.

When Lucy thought something was strange, she kept asking me all these things I was supposed to know but didn't. So maybe the proof is the opposite: everything I *do* know. Things I know that Cat wouldn't. I can tell her the price of a loaf of bread, a quart of milk or a pound of butter in 1908. The weather on the day I left, who the prime minister is, and how girls get on with things every month when they're on the rag. Things Cat has never thought about. (Things she might be thinking about a lot more now.)

Lucy takes a bite of her sandwich and lies stretched out like a starfish on the grass.

'It's nice to have you back again, Cat,' she says. 'After you went all strange.'

'Mm,' I say, waiting for my moment to tell her.

'It's so good to have a friend who gets me. Maybe I can help you with your stuff, too. Just ask, okay? Anything.'

Poor Lucy. I feel like her brain might break if I tell her about time travel. Is there a way I can get her help without scaring her too much?

'Are you any good with watches, Lucy?' I ask, reaching into my schoolbag. I dangle the stopwatch by the chain over her head and she reaches up for it. 'I need help with this old one.'

'I don't know that much about them, but there's an

insect called *Issus coleoptratus* that has legs just like the cogs inside a clock. What needs fixing on this one? Looks perfect to me.'

'That's just it. It was broken and I need it to be broken again. Before, the long, thin hand which is the timer hand was going anticlockwise. I want it to do that.'

Lucy frowns. 'You want me to help you break an antique.'

I nod and offer her a strawberry from my lunchbox. 'Yes, please,' I say. 'As soon as possible.'

31

Waiting

I'm in a chair by the stove with a blanket around my shoulders. Mary puts another one over my legs and kisses the top of my head. Dewey sits at my feet, takes my hands into hers and rubs them. I've been dry and dressed for ages but I can't seem to stop shaking or get warm.

No one in the kitchen is talking much. Just because Arthur got Frankie to cough up some water and breathe again doesn't mean it's over. People can drown hours after being pulled out of the water if too much of it has got into their lungs. So Doctor Burke is here and the last thing we heard him say was *I can't make any promises.*

I watch Con take a teapot from the shelf. His hands are shaking so much that the lid is rattling—Kath takes it off him and, empty-handed, Con goes to stand by the doorway that leads down to the yard, with his back to the room. It's easy to tell that he's crying.

Every time I glance at Da's grey face, I picture Ma and Da this morning, so happy to be treating everyone to a day out. And I think of my own mum and dad, working to make our lives happy. I can feel hot tears on my cheeks too.

John comes into the kitchen. 'Da,' he says in a strained voice. 'Father Robert is here.' The priest. Oh no, does that mean Frankie is going to die?

We're standing around Ma and Da's bed. I'm closest to the door. I want to be here but a part of me thinks I shouldn't be. This morning we were sitting in church listening to Father Robert talking about the joy of Sunday, and I wished time would speed up so we could get to the beach. Now all I want is for time to go back to the moment Frankie and Mick ran into the water.

Of all people I should know that time isn't something I can control. But is this my fault? Would the real Fan have reached him faster? Swimming isn't just about the body you're in; it's your mind too.

The priest is muttering prayers. Each face looking down at Frankie, who is swallowed up in the big bed, pale and still.

Then there's a little cough and a voice. 'Ma?'

His eyes open a little.

'Oh, Frankie!' Ma cries. Doctor Burke holds her

back and checks Frankie's chest, peels his eyelids back and feels around his throat.

He takes Ma's hands. 'Mrs Durack, I believe now that he'll pull through.'

'Oh! Doctor!' Ma's voice rings out like a bell. 'Really and truly?'

'His fever has dropped, his breathing sounds good. As best as I can tell, yes.' Doctor Burke nods and Ma flings her arms around him. The room comes to life with sound and movement as everyone hugs the person next to them. But I slink backwards through the doorway, breathing hard with relief and leftover shock. He's okay. He's really okay!

Dewey follows me out and we grip each other's hands. Silently we go into our bedroom and sit on the edge of our bed.

'Cat,' she whispers. 'You and Arthur saved him.'

I cry with relief but I can't speak because it's Fanny's voice that will come out and I think now, more than ever, I need to hear the sound of my own. I need to be myself again, so much.

'Cat, I just wish…'

I nod and squeeze her hand. She doesn't have to finish. She means that she needs her sister here. And I need mine! I've never wanted to hug that cheerful little cowpat more than I do right now. I even miss her stupid chicken alarm clock and the way she arranges her cozzie and shoes on the rug at night.

I know what else I miss. I miss knowing exactly what I want and why. I haven't felt that for such a long time, but it's never been clearer than it is today. I want my own life back and I know what I want to do with it, too.

It feels like the first big decision I've ever made by myself.

'You really want to go home, don't you?' says Dewey.

'I want to go and I want to give Fan back to you,' I answer.

Then as she puts her arms around me, we cry and laugh at the same time.

'I wish I could have both of you,' she sobs.

'I'm really not a crier, you know.'

Dewey laughs. 'Fanny's not a crier either.'

As we break apart, we catch sight of ourselves in the mirror on top of the dresser and laugh at how red and puffy our faces are.

'I need a handkerchief,' says Dewey.

'Oh, I've got one.' I slide open the drawer next to our bed and find the crumpled handkerchief with A.G. embroidered on it.

'Is this Arthur's?' Dewey gasps.

'He gave it to me the first day I got here.'

She holds it, feeling the fabric as if it's something

special. I'm sure we're both picturing the scene on the beach when Frankie's cold body was laid down on the sand and Arthur breathed life into him. And the next moment when Arthur was pushed aside, which was so unfair.

'It was a sign, Arthur giving you this,' says Dewey.

'And now we need another,' I add. 'We need a sign from Fanny.'

32
Relay

After school, Maisy and I play Monopoly with Mum. It's a strange game where people try to take each other's money. Then all four of us catch the tram into the city and go to Chinatown. Mum orders us fat steaming dumplings that dribble juice down my chin as I bite into them.

In my time, nobody from Irish stock would venture into a Chinese eating place and sit at tables alongside people speaking in foreign languages. I soak it up, keen to remember as much as I can. I can't manage chopsticks but I eat twenty-three dumplings and only stop because Dad refuses to buy more, worried that I'll burst.

Maisy asks about Lucy's protest and when I explain, Mum says Lucy is right to make a big deal about inclusion. It makes me wonder what Ma would say if I started to protest against girls and women being told that it's not right to swim in major competitions just because men will see them in bathing suits. More than ever, I want to get back to 1908 and fight my own battles.

'Put your phone away, Maisy,' says Dad, when he catches her tapping on it with her thumbs in that lightning-fast way she does. 'Cat, I've been meaning to say that it's really nice to see that you're not constantly glued to yours lately.'

I smile.

Maisy kicks me under the table.

The next morning Dad drops us off at training at 5.45 am, which means we're late. Rebecca is probably already in the pool. Maisy rushes through the turnstile in front of me. There's a week to go before Saturday's relay race.

Maisy gets ready in record time and leaves the dressing room tucking her hair up inside her swimming cap, another modern revelation.

'I'll see you out there, Maisy,' I tell her.

'You'd better hurry. Coach won't be happy!'

At Wylie's Baths, I'm the first in. This morning I'm stalling. I haven't mastered freestyle and I don't want to bring shame on Cat. As much as I could take Rebecca down a notch or two in breaststroke, something is stopping me.

I pull on Cat's bathing suit, loving the tight feel of it

against my skin. Unlike baggy wool, this fabric doesn't itch in places where it shouldn't. I don't bother with a cap. Cat's hair is short enough and I've always liked the swampy feel of the water in my hair. On the way out, I stop at the mirror. I stare deep into Cat's eyes, hoping she's looking after things for me and that she'll be ready to swap back when I am. A strange shiver of cold flushes through my body like someone has stepped across my grave. Ma would say I was coming down with something, but it's not like that. It's a different sort of feeling. It's like Cat is telling me that she's ready.

I push open the door to the pool.

'Nice of you to join us, Cat,' says Rebecca, bobbing up out of the water at the end of the lane. I ignore her because Kath taught me the power of that a long time ago. Rebecca sighs and swims away.

Maisy is in the water already and I stand watching her arms draw perfectly through the water. I imagine what my coach Mr Wylie would say if he could see her. Her body arches and she comes up for a breath and then slides back under. Her stroke is perfect. She hits the end, turns gracefully beneath the water and glides for a few seconds before popping back up again.

'She's good,' says a voice behind me.

I turn to find Coach in her wheelchair.

'She is,' I say.

'Better than you?' she asks.

'Today she is,' I say, not quite willing to accept I couldn't beat Maisy in my own body, in my own stroke.

'Well, are you getting in or not, Cat?'

Maisy touches the end and changes strokes. My heart is racing like it does before I swim, when my lungs are trying to take in all the air they can. I know what I have to do. I just hope that Cat forgives me.

'Coach, I think you should put Maisy in the relay team instead of me. She's faster than me at the moment, and she wants it more.'

Coach comes closer and stares at me. It's so intimidating. Here I was thinking Mr Wylie was a little frightening, but he has nothing on this coach.

'What about your scholarship?'

I haven't thought this through. I'm not sure what Cat wants, but I do know that I would never pretend to be sick to miss training, and if my parents moved me to a new town and a new school so that I had a better shot of making the Olympics, I would take it in a flash. From everything Maisy has said, Cat wants something else.

But what if I'm wrong? Or if I can't go back to my time?

'I need time to think. I'll have all the answers soon. Please don't say anything to my mother and father yet.'

Coach frowns. 'Last chance, Cat.'

I nod. 'I know. Thank you. Don't be disappointed in me, Coach.'

'You're young. You've got a big life ahead of you. Let's talk when you're ready. Now, are you getting in this water today or not?'

I look at all the squad lanes and I want that feeling that I can only get from a good swim.

'I'm going to work on my breaststroke, if that's all right with you, Coach.'

She nods and gestures to the far lane.

There are only two other girls so I wait for the right moment and start my first lap.

I chase the girl in front of me and wait for that moment when my body remembers it's a sea creature and every movement in water feels more natural than when I'm on land. I'm quick and strong. Coming up to the end I take one big breath before diving down and turning over, kicking off the wall sleek as anyone in this squad. I use the underwater kick that I watched Maisy do, which has never been used in my time for racing.

Why ease a spate...

It's the whisper! I gasp for air when I break the surface and plunge back down to hear it again. It didn't make any sense! *Why ease a spate?* What does that mean? I hold my breath and pray I hear it again.

While e's are straight...

What the devil? Whisper again, Cat! I don't understand!

Wylie's at eight…

Oh! Of course that's what it is! Wylie's Baths at eight o'clock.

I've got another half a lap to go and this time I don't care who sees me break into trudgen to get to the end. I have to get out of here and find Lucy.

PART 5

SPRINT

33

Synchronise

Cat

I look around the room, thinking: *what do I need?* But that's not how this works. Everything here is Fanny's.

Kath, Mary and Dewey are asleep. Too bad they're going to miss the one time I was up and dressed before them, but there are reasons I can't say goodbye. One is that they don't know that Fan hasn't been here this whole time. Another is that my new plan might not work today, or tomorrow, or the next day. But one day it will. I plan on swimming at Wylie's every morning until it does. Without a sign from Fanny about whether she's found Aunt Rachel's stopwatch, or proof that she's in my place, there's nothing else I can do but get up at dawn and swim.

I've got Fan's carpetbag, money for the tram (not stolen this time), the stopwatch, and a shawl in case it's cold when Fan gets back. *If* she gets back. I'm fizzing with excitement when I shouldn't be, but I can't help it!

As I sneak along the hall, I peek into Ma and Da's bedroom. They're in bed, with Frankie in between them, all fast asleep. I keep going, touching the bedroom door where Con and John sleep, and next to that Mick's room that he usually shares with his little brother. I found him crying in there last night after we'd found out that Frankie was going to be all right—he'd bottled it all up until then.

I creep through the kitchen and across the backyard.

I'm opening the door to the laneway when I hear Ma's voice.

'Sarah Francis Durack, where d'you think you're off to?' She's standing at the top of the yard steps, rubbing sleep from her eyes.

'Just for a walk, Ma.'

'With a bag?'

'Um, I…accidentally took Mina Wylie's swimming robe after the race. I need to return it to her.'

'What, all the way to Coogee? After the day we had yesterday?' She starts down the steps.

I can't let her drag me back. 'Ma, I promise I'll be back soon.'

When she reaches me, she looks at me with her inscrutable face, then nods sharply. 'Now, listen here, Fan. I know what you're sneaking off for. A mother knows. I've had my doubts about you and swimming, can't deny it. But I won't do or say a single thing to get in your way from now on. Whatever you need, my girl. You got that?'

'Yes, Ma.'

A sudden shiver makes my body jolt.

'You're cold, Fan! Gracious, we've been worrying all this time about Frankie and you could have pneumonia yourself.'

'I'm not cold! I promise, Ma. It was just one of those strange shivers.' I wonder what that shiver means. Could it be a sign? 'I've never felt better, Ma. Honest.'

She pulls me into her arms and I feel myself melt a little. Strong, hardworking Ma. Who knows what she could have been if she'd been born in 2008, like I was.

'Thanks for everything, Ma. I love you all.'

She holds me at arm's length and gives me a suspicious look. 'I think the shock of yesterday has turned you soft, Fanny Durack.'

'Not a chance,' I reply.

I'm stepping onto the Coogee tram when I hear a shout.

'Wait for me!'

Dewey jumps on and plonks down next to me. Her eyes are shining and she's out of breath.

'Couldn't…let you go…alone,' she says, panting.

'How did you know? You were fast asleep when I snuck out.'

'You're noisier than you think. And you were talking in your sleep again. I heard you in the night so I knew you had a plan.'

'What was I saying?'

'"Wylie's at eight." Over and over. I can't believe you were going to go without me.'

'I don't even know if it will work, Dew. I might have to do this every single morning for…years.'

Dewey shakes her head. 'I don't think so. I had a feeling when I woke up that Fan was coming home today. And you know I'm good at feelings—I figured *you* out.'

'True,' I smile. But I feel sad in a way, thinking about Fan and Dewey seeing each other again. Before this happened, I felt so alone in my thoughts. As if I was stuck inside them. Am I going back to more of that?

I shiver again, my arms and legs jerking like a puppet.

'What was that?' says Dewey.

'I don't know. Maybe just a shiver, maybe a sign?'

'Da says a big shiver like that means someone's walked over your grave.'

'I don't have a grave,' I reply with a frown.

'Well, Da doesn't know everything, I suppose.' She links her arm in mine and squeezes closer.

Fan

Lucy is where Lucy always is. In the lab, white coat on, hair up, and looking serious. I watch her from the small window as she leans over the microscope, lost to another world.

'Morning,' I say pushing open the door.

'What are you doing here? Aren't you supposed to be training?'

'I've got somewhere else I need to be, and I wondered if you'd had any luck with that stopwatch.'

Lucy reaches into her lab coat.

'Oh, this stopwatch? You will never believe what I did.'

'Tell me!' I try to snatch it but she laughs and holds it out of my reach. 'Lucy!'

'All right, but listen. I spent all night studying the *Issus coleoptraptus*.'

'The insect that has cogs like a watch.'

'Exactly. Humans have always believed that cogs were invented by the Greeks in the third century, and that's how we ended up with anything that uses gears, including clocks. But this insect uses cogs to make it jump. So I studied how that works to work out a way to undo the cogs.'

She stops, and has a look in the microscope in front of her.

'And?' I say. 'Lucy! Did it work or not?'

'Not,' she replies, and looks up again. 'But, on the way home, I dropped it and…look.' She holds it out. The long timer hand is sweeping around the face anticlockwise!

'You did it!'

I grab the watch and kiss her on the cheek.

She wipes it off, laughing. 'Well, lots of scientific discoveries happened by accident.'

'I'm so grateful, Lucy.'

'It was the weirdest request I've ever had, but I'm happy if you're happy.'

I take a longer look at the stopwatch, and find it difficult to look away. I have thoughts half-formed in my mind that I want to tell Lucy, but I'm transfixed by the hand spinning backwards. Even after I start to feel dizzy, I keep looking.

'Cat?' Lucy puts her hand over the watch face.

'Sorry, I was just…having a strange moment.'

'Are you okay?'

'I'm grand. I have to go. I need to…do an experiment.'

She scowls and clutches her white lab coat tighter as if it's keeping her safe from my strange ideas. 'Right. I have double maths first and I categorically cannot be late.'

I pull out a chocolate honeycomb bar that my new

mother gave me from her travels because we didn't have time to make lunch this morning. 'Here,' I say holding it out to her.

'You know how I feel about honeycomb.'

The thing is I don't even know how I feel about honeycomb because I've never had it before.

'Bye, Lucy,' I say.

'See you at recess. Usual place?'

I nod and smile as I push open the lab door.

Cat

The water looks like ink from up here. It's a cloudy morning, not much wind, no sun.

'It's nice to think that these baths will still be here in more than a hundred years,' says Dewey. 'Does it look the same?'

I think back to the day the swap happened. Walking down the concrete stairs, dropping the money in the tray. The cafe, the people. The statue of a girl looking out to—oh! I've realised who that statue is. It's Mina Wylie! It makes sense that it's her as this is her father's place. But I wonder if that means that Mina Wylie is the one who becomes a famous swimmer and not Fanny. So I don't mention the statue to Dewey.

'Almost the same,' I reply, and I feel the shiver again.

'Another shiver?' Dewey asks. 'Maybe that means

my sister is here too.' She looks down at the baths as if Fan might appear. 'Come on, let's try,' Dewey says. She is so sure, and I wish I could be too.

In the changing rooms, Dewey starts to strip off as well. She catches me frowning.

'Don't worry, I know I can't come to your time. I just want to watch it happen. I won't get into the water until we're sure. Please let me be part of it.'

'I want you there, Dew. It's just that I was alone when it happened before. Wait, no, there was an old lady in the water at the same time.'

'Maybe she was an enchanter,' says a wide-eyed Dewey, making the Catholic sign of the cross.

I laugh. But I'm not positive she's wrong.

The water's so cold that I make funny noises getting into it. Dewey has the stopwatch and she's standing at the edge, exactly where she was the first time I ever saw her.

The next shiver is a huge one. I float on my back and try to feel at home in the water.

'Tell me about that day again,' says Dewey.

'Well, I was angry with everyone. I wanted to escape.'

'Is that how you feel now?'

'I'm not angry with anyone. Here or there.'

'Did you think you wanted to get away from

everything for good?'

'I wanted to escape some of my life, but not all of it.'

'And now you want to escape 1908, even though you will be sorry to leave some of it behind.'

I nod, and bite my lip.

We're quiet for a while. *Ssshhh*, goes the ocean. I dip my head right back in the water and feel the weight of Fanny's hair as I stand up again.

'It's time, Cat,' says Dewey.

Fan

The bus jolts to a stop near Wylie's Baths. I reach up and press the button, alight from the bus and hurry across the road. My heart is tripping over itself to reach the water, and I hope I'm not misreading these shivery moments.

I rush down the stairs to the baths. There's no sign this time stopping me from entering, and I dig in my pocket for coins to place in the turnstile. It's like I'm about to swim a race in front of Da. That's how excited I feel.

The place is almost empty, except for a couple of lizard-looking men sunbaking in their little pants. I go to the exact rocks where we found Cat's bag, and there I undress, taking a moment to fold up Cat's tracksuit. Then I sit down and take out the stopwatch.

Watching its unwinding hand is like being entranced.

I feel so giddy and slow I don't know if I can stand up. I'm sure this is it.

I put the stopwatch on Cat's folded clothes and lower Cat's goggles over my eyes. I want to see the dancing coloured coral and the darting fish as I try to swim home.

Climbing fast down the metal ladder, I push off into the coolness of salty clean water hoping that somehow Cat is doing the same.

I swim trudgen—my stroke—and stare down into the depths, still seeing that unwinding hand in my mind's eye.

Cat

My heart rate is as rapid as if I'm in a race. *Calm down*, I tell myself. I open my eyes cautiously and find they can take the saltwater. Four kicks in, I'm ready, and I come to the surface to begin freestyle.

I slip into it easily, and think of yesterday when I was swimming through the waves to save Frankie. Stroke-stroke breathe, stroke-stroke breathe.

'Good luck, Cat!' Dewey calls.

Good luck to you too, I think. And to Arthur, and Mary and Kath and Mina, little Frankie and Mick, lovely Con and unfun John. Ma and Da.

But what if…

What if…

What if I can't…

I keep my head down. It's dark ahead—I wish I could see the wall.

Just keep swimming, just keep swimming.

I hold my arms in front of me and kick as hard as I can.

Fan

My fingers graze the hard grey stone.

My fingers! They are *my* fingers. My hand. My hair hangs long and thick over my face. I pat my skin. It's me. It's my strong muscled body and I'm wearing my baggy heavy bathing suit.

'Fanny? *Fanny!*'

My name. I look up to see who is calling me. There's a girl standing at the other end. It's my Dewey.

I squeal out her name and she calls mine again.

I swim towards her, the saltwater stinging my eyes, and my legs heavy as they kick. This body hasn't been training hard. I can feel it in my muscles as I pull through the water.

Dewey is pacing back and forth at the edge, like she's about to hurl herself in. Does she know that I've been gone?

I rush for the stairs and Dewey is there, at the top,

with her arms out, and her face lit in the broadest of grins.

'It's you,' she says. She knows. I bury myself in her hug, and I'm home.

Cat

I stand up when I feel a tightness around my face.

Goggles!

I whip them off and touch the short hair at the back of my neck.

I'm me!

Squinting into a low morning sun, I can see Coogee Beach in the distance, a surfer on a wave. The hills rise up behind the beach and there are high-rise apartments, dozens of rooftops—a helicopter! Yes, I'm back.

I look behind me and there are about a dozen people all getting ready for a swim, but no one yet in the water. And no one I know. It's so strange. I'm alone, but I'm home, and that feels amazing.

Straightaway I see my stuff—it's piled neatly on the same rock where I left my bag that day. Someone must have done that for me. Was it Fanny Durack?

I spy the stopwatch and pick it up. It's tarnished and dented and the face isn't as pristine as it was in 1908. The hands are completely still, fixed on the nine and the four, looking like a diver.

PART 6

FINISH

34
Home

Dewey's favourite stories are the ones I tell her about living above a shop and eating lollies and potato scallops and worms in sauce from a tin. She has funny stories for me too, about Cat and her strange ways.

Cat saved my brother, and for that we'll be connected forever. She left me a note that was hard to read because of her handwriting. But Dewey and I worked it out together. Dewey smiled at the thought of Cat liking her. I told her nobody could ever not like her.

Dewey has more questions for me every day and I never tire of answering them. It keeps a part of my time in the future alive inside me, that little part that reminds me that one day women wear whatever they like, and work wherever they like, and swim for their country. And that all that will happen if women like me, here and now, go into battle to change things.

I wonder about Cat and Maisy, and if Cat has

decided to stay in her squad and be a swimmer after all. I wonder about Lucy and her fight to get a place on the science course. But mostly, I wonder about my future. Will I swim for my country? Will Da ever watch me race? Will things change?

'Fanny! There are rabbits to skin, stop daydreaming,' yells Ma from the kitchen.

One thing that will never change is Ma yelling orders.

'I'm here, Ma,' I say. 'I have to train later but I can start on dinner before I go.'

She sighs and I wait for the grumbling to start about swimming, but she just hands me the rabbit knife and the board.

'Need any help, Fan?' Dewey asks, dropping a load of wood near the fire.

'No, dear Dewey. I've missed skinning rabbits!'

My sister laughs and gets started on the potatoes.

'No larking, you two. I want this on the cooker by the time I'm back,' Ma says.

'Yes, Ma.'

'You look nice today, Ma,' I say, noticing that she has colour on her cheeks and her hair off her face.

'I'm going into town.'

'Alone?' Dewey says.

Ma scoffs, like the idea is ridiculous. I want to tell

her that in the future she could go to work and Da could do the cooking, but she'd probably whisk me off to hospital for having daft notions.

'With your father. We're meeting his cousin,' says Ma, brushing down her Sunday coat.

'Have fun, Ma!' I call as she leaves, and Dewey gives me a sharp look because I've done it again, used words from the wrong time. But Ma's too preoccupied to notice and we hear her best shoes clip and clop down the stairs to the pub.

'Tell me the story about the party in Rebecca's house and the raw fish,' Dewey says quietly.

'Again?'

She nods.

'Sashimi, it's called,' I say, as I launch into the story of the posh house on the hill. Dewey forgets that she's supposed to be peeling potatoes and sits with her head on her hands to listen.

My little sister has a worried look. 'Fan, are you happy to be back?' Her voice is shaky, like she's had to work up the courage to ask.

I don't answer straightaway. There are things I'll miss, like the freedoms of dressing without corsets and layers. The idea I can swim whenever I like, travel the world, and put dirty clothes into a washing machine and then press one button to do all the work.

But the sight of Dewey tugs me back to my home and my noisy, funny family who love me and support me and let me be me. My own people and my own time.

'Yes. I am happy to be back. It's *awesome*,' I say, trying out a word I know my sister will never have heard before. But she giggles. 'Cat said that. It means really, really great.'

She jumps up and pulls me into a Dewey hug that is just about the best thing in the entire world.

35
Home

About an hour ago I found my laptop and phone under my bed in a large tray of rice. The laptop is lifeless. RIP me when my parents find out, but by some miracle the phone just started working again.

Ping-ping-ping-ping-ping! Texts from everyone in Orange. Alerts telling me I've been tagged in a photo. Reminders for homework I was meant to have finished. It's overwhelming watching them all rush in.

I take a deep breath and remind myself that the messages can wait a little bit longer.

The first hours of my return have been really strange. I managed to get through a whole day of school without seeing my sister, and she wasn't at the bus stop after school so I travelled home alone, feeling strange and nervous.

When I walked into the shop, Dad was there, restocking the shelves. I had to keep swallowing to stop myself from crying. There was no way I wanted to tell my family that I'd been sucked into 1908. I mean, they'd *never* let me out again! And I'd come back with big plans about how I was going to spend my time. So I kissed Dad on the cheek, helped myself to a potato scallop from the bain-marie, and didn't say a word.

When Maisy finally walks into our bedroom later, she has a funny look on her face. Well, not so much funny as petrified.

'What?' I say.

'Err...Cat...'

'Yeaaahhh?'

'Coach seems to think that you don't want your place in the relay team anymore and that I should take it but I told her *no way* Cat would *never* say that Cat's just been feeling *strange* lately but she'll be *fine* and there's no way I could take her place no way *never.*'

'Breathe, Maise.'

She takes a deep, shuddery breath. I smile. Fanny must have realised how I felt. She'd done me a favour, breaking the news to Coach. I wonder if I would have done it myself when it came to it.

Yes, I definitely would have.

I get up from the bed and go over to my sister, who actually flinches. 'Am I really that scary?' I say.

'Cat, you're my sister. I love you. But yes, you are.'

'Come here,' I say, hooking my arm around her neck and pulling her close to me. 'I'm sorry I've been a cowpat.'

'You haven't, *lately.*'

'Mm. Well, I mean before.' I guess that Fanny had been lovely to everyone, and I am probably going to die of exhaustion over the next few weeks trying to be as nice as her.

Then again, Dewey thought I was nice in 1908. So did Mary and Kath. And Mina, and Arthur and Con. And Ma and Da. Maybe even unfun John, in the end. That was all me.

'I want you to have that relay place, Maise. You're a great swimmer and you deserve it. You do want it, don't you?'

'But don't *you?*' Maisy says, pulling away. 'What's happened to you, Cat?'

I feel a bit like a ghost, but gradually I'm coming back to life. I'm in the kitchen now, making a surprise dinner for everyone—well, it's frozen pizza, but I'm the one putting it in the oven.

I hear the door bang downstairs, and footsteps.

'Mum's here!' calls Maisy from the other room.

My heart catches. It's been so long since I've seen her. As I listen to Maisy swamp Mum with hugs and questions in the hallway, I look at the table I've laid.

I've put cherry blossoms in a washed-out jam jar. I just can't wait for us to be together. Once we're all sitting down, I'm going to tell Mum and Dad that I want to drop my scholarship—Maisy can take it up, I hope.

And then I'll tell them I want to get my Surf Rescue Certificate. I've done all the research, I can do it at Coogee. That way I'll always remember exactly why I'm doing it. Frankie was my first rescue but he won't be my last. I *know* that this is what I want to do.

'Well, it's good to be home,' says my beautiful mum as she walks into the kitchen.

She holds out her arms, and finally, *finally*, they're wrapped around me.

Afterword

The Real Sarah 'Fanny' Durack

Some of this story was drawn from real historical facts. Sarah Frances Durack, known to friends and family as Fanny, was born in 1889. She lived above the Newmarket Pub in Sydney with her parents, Tommy and Mary, and her siblings: John, Thomas, Kathleen, Mary, Cornelius (Con), Julia (Dewey), Mick and Frank.

When Fanny was nine years old she was knocked down by a wave and rescued by a St Bernard dog. After that, her father made her join Sydney's only bathing establishment for girls, in Coogee. Tommy paid the entry fee but couldn't afford lessons, so Fanny just watched and taught herself dog paddle.

Fanny's friend and rival Wilhelmina (Mina) Wylie was born in 1891. Mina's father, Henry, a champion swimmer, built Wylie's Baths in 1907. Fanny and Mina were keen lifesavers, among the first women to become fully qualified.

In 1912 there was a long, public fight about sending Fanny and Mina to the Olympics to represent Australia. Some argued that women swimming in front of men was immoral. Fanny and Mina fought hard and finally won the right to go. On 15 July 1912, Fanny became the first Australian woman to win Olympic gold at a swimming event. Mina won silver.

Fanny's family lived in the pub for many years. Dewey married a boxer named Jimmy Hill in 1912. They moved to America, so Dewey did get her own adventure after all.

Finally, you can still go swimming at Wylie's Baths in Coogee. We did!

Emily & Nova

Acknowledgments

First, we would like to thank Fanny Durack and Mina Wylie and the other women swimmers of their time, who fought hard for the right to swim and compete as freely as men. These women were fiercely strong and determined, and our wish for this book is that they will be rediscovered.

When we sent *Elsewhere Girls* to Jane Pearson at Text, her reaction was the best a writer could hope for. A huge thanks to Jane and everyone at Text for embracing this story with passion. Thanks to Malgosia Pietowska for the exquisite cover art and to Imogen Stubbs for the lovely design, which makes us both want to dive into Wylie's Baths again.

Thanks to Aidan Fennessy, who told us early on that we must include the voice of Fanny in the chapters and consequently changed the book completely. Once we explored her life and heard her voice on the page, the story started to breathe.

Thanks to the librarians at various libraries in Sydney who helped us find rare, archived boxes of treasures, like the old posters advertising swimming meets at Lavender Bay Baths in the early 1900s.

Thanks to swimming coach Damien Gogoll, who generously shared information about training sessions and his coaching philosophy. Any errors are our own.

Thanks to the authors who have come before us, writing time-slip and body-swap novels that we have both loved. *Freaky Friday*, *Charlotte Sometimes*, *Playing Beattie Bow*: these books loomed large in our childhoods and it's been such a treat to write one of our own.

And finally, it might sound a little odd to thank each other, but this book was an act of friendship. Co-writing can be a tricky adventure, but in the case of *Elsewhere Girls* it was a dream. We chose a character each (you'll have to guess which). We plotted together, wrote alternating chapters and sent them back and forth like letters. Writing can be lonely; co-writing this book was anything but.